ECONOMICS QUIZ

Professor A. N. Agarwal taught economics for over forty years before retiring from Ramjas College, Delhi. He is the author of *India Quiz*.

ECONOMICS QUIZ

A. N. AGARWAL

RUPA

Published by
Rupa Publications India Pvt. Ltd. 1991
7/16, Ansari Road, Daryaganj
New Delhi 110002

Sales centres:

Allahabad Bengaluru Chennai
Hyderabad Jaipur Kathmandu
Kolkata Mumbai

Cover design by M. Mallick

ISBN: 978-81-716-7060-4

Eighth impression 2019

15 14 13 12 11 10 9 8

The moral right of the author has been asserted.

Preface

The Oxford Reference Dictionary defines a quiz as a 'series of questions testing people's knowledge as a form of entertainment'. The entertainment aspect of quizzing certainly cannot be doubted. And it is this feature which largely accounts for its growing popularity at various forums such as schools, colleges, clubs and television. Nonetheless, quizzing has acquired over a period of time a dimension of seriousness and sobriety. The format of questioning even at high levels of testing for recruitment to civil and other services is steadily acquiring the flavour of quizzing over a large expanse of diverse subjects. Since these tests have a competitive character, those subjected to these questions cannot but view the exercise seriously.

A quiz on one specific subject has, however, the added flavours questioning about the depth of knowledge and understanding of the subject under consideration. The present quiz book is concerned with Economics — an exciting and highly popular subject both at different levels of education and competitive examinations. It consists of one thousand carefully formulated and suitably graded questions from the two main branches of Economics, viz., Micro-economics and Macro-economics. The fields covered extend from the well-known economists and their works, glimpses of world economy, international economic organisation, national income accounting and growth and development to demand, supply and price, business and finance, economic and commercial geography, and money, banking and international trade. About one-fourth of questions touch upon the main facets of the Indian economy — its institutional framework, the economic scenario and planning and development.

The book is so designed as to enable the readers to list their grasp over the fundamentals of the subject as also stimulate the desire to know still more of it. Apart from general readers and students at different levels, the candidates appearing at the various competitive examinations will find the book interesting and highly useful.

I must thank Dr Hari Om Varma and Shri Vivek Kuchhal for their valuable assistance. Special thanks are due to my wife, Savitri Agarwal, for her great care and encouragement. I must also thank my grand-daughter Ruchira Agarwal, for her help in preparing the final draft.

Delhi
April 1991   A N Agarwal

Contents

I
GREAT ECONOMISTS AND THEIR WORK

1. In which year was Francois Quesnay's *Tableu Economique* published?
   (a) 1767 (b) 1764 (c) 1761 (d) 1758
2. Identify the author of *The Principles of Political Economy and Taxation:*
   (a) Alfred Marshall (b) J.S. Mill
   (c) David Ricardo (d) A. Turgot
3. Who is generally regarded as the founder of the Classical School?
   (a) David Ricardo (b) Adam Smith
   (c) T.R. Malthus (d) J.S. Mill
4. Identify the economist who had little formal education and started working in the money market at an early age of fourteen:
   (a) David Ricardo (b) Adam Smith
   (c) V.F.D. Pareto (d) A.A. Cournot
5. "The labour of Nature is paid, not because she does much, but because she does little. In proportion as she becomes niggardly in her gifts, she exacts a greater price for her work." Who made this observation?
   (a) Adam Smith (b) T.R. Malthus
   (c) David Ricardo (d) Lauderdale
6. Who first raised fears of a world food shortage?
   (a) David Ricardo (b) T.R. Malthus
   (c) J.S. Mill (d) J.B. Say
7. When was Adam Smith's major work *An Enquiry into the Nature and Causes of Wealth of Nations* published?

1

(a) 1756 (b) 1766 (c) 1776 (d) 1786

8. "The real price of every thing, what every thing really costs to the man who wants to require it, is the toil and trouble of acquiring it." Who made this statement?
(a) Karl Marx (b) Adam Smith (c) David Ricardo (d) J.S. Mill

9. "Rent is a creation of value, not of wealth." Who made this observation?
(a) Adam Smith (b) David Ricardo (c) Alfred Marshall (d) A.C. Pigou

10. In which year was the first volume of *Das Capital* by Karl Marx published?
(a) 1848 (b) 1859 (c) 1867 (d) 1873

11. The *Critique of Political Economy*, the first fruits of Karl Marx's long painstaking research at the British Museum, appeared in:
(a) 1859 (b) 1857 (c) 1855 (d) 1853

12. The *Communist Manifesto*, written jointly by Marx and Engels, was published in:
(a) 1843 (b) 1848 (c) 1853 (d) 1859

13. Who stated explicitly for the first time the law of comparative costs?
(a) David Ricardo (b) Adam Smith (c) James Mill (d) Thomas Mun

14. Identify the school founded by Wilhelm Roscher:
(a) Austrian School (b) Historical School (c) Cambridge School (d) Mathematical School

15. One of the following economists do not belong to the Austrian School. Identify him:
(a) J.S. Mill (b) Karl Menger (c) F. von Wieser (d) E. von Böhm-Bawerk

16. Which one of the following theories of trade cycle was propounded by W.S. Jevons?

(a) Sunspot Theory (b) Monetary Theory (c) Saving-Investment Theory (d) Innovation Theory

17. What was the nationality of Frederich List?
    (a) American (b) German (c) British (d) Finnish

18. The Purchasing Power Parity Theory came into prominence in 1916 through the writings of:
    (a) J.M. Keynes (b) L.E. von Miser (c) Gustav Cassel (d) F.A. von Hayek

19. The input-output analysis owes its origin and development to:
    (a) W.W. Leontief (b) R.F. Harrod (c) E.D. Domar (d) Alfred Marshall

20. Who wrote *An Introduction to Positive Economics*?
    (a) R.G. Lipsey (b) Paul A. Samuelson (c) G.B. Richardson (d) W.J. Baumol

21. Identify the author of *Mathematical Analysis for Economists:*
    (a) J.P. Lewis (b) R.G.D. Allen (c) Russel Mathews (d) B.J. Cohen

22. Which of the following is not correctly matched?
    (a) Lionel Robbins: *The Great Depression*
    (b) D.H. Robertson: *Essays in Monetary Theory*
    (c) A.C. Pigou: *Principles and Methods of Industrial Peace* (d) R.F. Harrod: *Income and Money*

23. Who among the following well-known economists graduated from the London School of Economics?
    (a) J.M. Keynes (b) N. Kaldor (c) Alfred Marshall (d) F.A. Hayek

3

24. The *Strategy of Economic Development* is the work of:
    (a) S. Kuznets (b) H. Liebenstein (c) H. Myint (d) A.O. Hirshman

25. Who is the author of *Problems of Capital Formation in Underdeveloped Countries?*
    (a) R. Nurkse (b) N. Kaldor (c) S. Kuznets (d) J.N. Bhagwati

26. Identify the work of Irving Fisher:
    (a) *A Treatese on Money* (b) *Policy Against Inflation* (c) *The Making of Index Numbers* (d) *Monetary Theory*

27. Who wrote "There are no longer any believers in *laissez-faire* except on the lunatic fringe—the truth is that we are all planners now"?
    (a) E.F. Durbin (b) H.R. Dickenson (c) W.A. Lewis (d) J. Tinbergen

28. Who coined the phrase 'a temporary abode of purchasing power' while explaining the concept of money?
    (a) Francis Walker (b) Milton Friedman (c) D.H. Robertson (d) J.M. Keynes

29. Who developed the Keynesian Theory of Distribution?
    (a) J.M. Keynes (b) N. Kaldor (c) C.P. Kindleberger (d) Joan Robinson

30. Identify the economist who propounded the Liquidity Preference Theory of Interest:
    (a) K. Wicksell (b) Nassau Senior (c) D.H. Robertson (d) J.M. Keynes

31. Which one among the following does not match?
    (a) Amartya Sen — Harvard (b) Jagdish Bhagwati — Princeton (c) T.N. Srinivasan — Yale (d) P.S. Dasgupta — Cambridge

32. Which of the following is not the work of J.B. Clark?
(a) *Philosophy of Wealth* (b) *The Control of Trusts* (c) *Economics of Overhead Costs* (d) *The Problem of Monopoly*

33. Identify the economist who propounded the Time Preference Theory of Interest:
(a) Nassau Senior (b) Böhm Bawerk (c) J.M. Keynes (d) K. Wicksell

34. Who developed the concept of representative firm?
(a) A.C. Pigou (b) Alfred Marshall (c) J.M. Keynes (d) A.W.H. Phillips

35. Identify the work of T. Schultz:
(a) *Transforming Traditional Agriculture* (b) *Productivity and Technical Change* (c) *Jobs, Poverty and the Green Revolution* (d) *The Green Revolution: Generations of Problems*

36. Which of the following does not match?
(a) J.R. Hicks: *Capital and Growth* (b) C.P. Kindleberger: *Economic Development* (c) H. Myint: *Economic Theory and Underdeveloped Regions* (d) E.H. Phelps-Brown: *The Economics of Labour*

37. Which of the following Alfred Marshall's works was first published?
(a) *The Pure Theory of Foreign Trade* (b) *The Principles of Economics* (c) *Industry and Trade* (d) *Money, Credit and Commerce*

38. Who first used the term 'quasi-rent'?
(a) David Ricardo (b) Alfred Marshall (c) J.S. Mill (d) Karl Marx

39. How old was Alfred Marshall when he died?
(a) 80 (b) 82 (c) 85 (d) 90

40. Among the following Noble Prize winners for Economics one is an Austrian economist. Identify him.
(a) George Stigler (b) F.A. von Hayek (c) Simon Kuznets (d) Herbert A. Simon

41. Who used the term *consumption capital* for consumers' goods?
(a) Karl Marx (b) W.S. Jevons (c) Alfred Marshall (d) M.E.L. Walras

42. Whose words are these?
"We might as reasonable dispute whether it is the upper or the under blade of a pair of scissors that cuts a piece of paper as whether value is governed by utility or cost of production."
(a) Alfred Marshall (b) W.S. Jevons (c) J.S. Mill (d) David Ricardo

43. Who introduced the concept of elasticity of demand into economic theory?
(a) K. Wicksell (b) Alfred Marshall (c) J.S. Mill (d) A.C. Pigou

44. Though the concept of consumers surplus can be traced back to the French engineer-economist Dupuit, it was another economist who gave a precise formulation stating the necessary assumption of this concept. Identify the economist.
(a) Alfred Marshall (b) W.S. Jevons (c) F.W. Taussig (d) J.S. Mill

45. Who succeeded Alfred Marshall as Professor of Political Economy at Cambridge?
(a) A.C. Pigou (b) D.H. Robertson (c) J.M. Keynes (d) F.H. Knight

46. Which one among the following does not match?

(a) Adam Smith — Classical School (b) Karl Menger — Austrian School (c) A.C. Pigou — Cambridge School (d) W.S. Jevons — Historical School

47. Identify the Indian economist who was given an honorary knighthood by the British Government in 1990 for his wide-ranging contribution to education, development economics and finance:
    (a) I.G. Patel (b) A.K. Sen (c) K.N. Raj (d) V.K.R.V. Rao

48. Identify the author of *Poverty and Un-British Rule in India*:
    (a) R.C. Dutt (b) Dadabhai Naoroji (c) Raja Rammohun Roy (d) Surendranath Banerjea

49. *Capital and Development Planning* is the work of:
    (a) S. Chakravarty (b) W.A. Lewis (c) A.K. Dasgupta (d) N. Kaldor

50. Who is the author of *Choice of Technique*?
    (a) K.N. Raj (b) Amartya Sen (c) W.B. Redaway (d) J.R. Harris

51. Identify the author of *Employment Aspects of Planning in Underdeveloped countries*:
    (a) R. Nurkse (b) G. Myrdal (c) K.N. Raj (d) W.A. Lewis

52. Identify the author of *The Trade Cycle*:
    (a) J.M. Clark (b) R.C. Mathews (c) A.H. Hansen (d) Maurice Dobb

53. The theory of Monopolistic Competition was developed in the 1930s almost simultaneously and independently by two well-known economists. One was E.H. Chamberlin Who was the other?

(a) Joan Robinson (b) Alfred Marshall
(c) J.K. Galbraith (d) A.C. Pigou

54. Which of the following is not the work of
J.A. Schumpeter?
(a) *Theory of Economic Development* (b) *Readings
in Economics* (c) *History of Economic Analysis*
(d) *Business Cycles*

55. Who is the author of *Capitalism, Yesterday and
Today*?
(a) Karl Marx (b) M. Dobb
(c) J.A. Schumpeter (d) J.K. Galbraith

56. Identify the work by Amartya Sen:
(a) *Employment, Technology and Development*
(b) *The Economics of Developing Countries*
(c) *India's Green Revolution: Economic Gains and
Political Costs* (d) *Land Reforms and Economic
Development*

57. Identify the nationality of the 1977 Economics
Noble Prize winner Bertil Ohlin:
(a) Swedish (b) Norwegian (c) German
(d) American

58. Which one of the following has been the most
influential work of F.H. Knight?
(a) *Freedom and Reform* (b) *The Economic Organisation* (c) *The Economic Order and Religion*
(d) *Risk, Uncertainty and Profit*

59. Who first formulated the Revealed Preference
Approach to free the theory of consumer behaviour from the constraint of traditional concept of utility?
(a) Paul A. Samuelson (b) John Robinson
(c) J.R. Hicks (d) R.G.D. Allen

60. Which of the following is the work of
E.H. Chamberlin?

(a) *Theory of Monopolistic Competition* (b) *Towards a more General Theory of Value* (c) *The Economic Analysis of Labour Union Power* (d) All of these

61. Identify the author of *The Social Framework*:
    (a) R.G.D. Allen (b) J.R. Hicks (c) R.F. Harrod
    (d) A.C. Pigou

62. Who in particular advocated the long-term capital gains tax?
    (a) J.M. Keynes (b) J.K. Galbraith
    (c) N. Kaldor (d) F.H. Knight

63. Which of the following is the work of Paul Baran?
    (a) *The Political Economy of Growth* (b) *Essays on Economic Planning* (c) *Economic Development*
    (d) *Soviet Economic Development since 1917*

64. With which of the following is the name of Jacob Viner associated?
    (a) Single factoral terms of trade (b) Utility terms of trade (c) Net barter terms of trade
    (d) Income terms of trade

65. Who first formulated the Marginal Productivity Theory of Distribution?
    (a) J.B. Clark (b) F.H. Knight
    (c) J.A. Schumpeter (d) L. Euler

66. Which one of the following is the work of A.C. Pigou?
    (a) *Economics of Welfare* (b) *Industry and Trade*
    (c) *Input-output Economics* (d) *Full Employment in a Free Society*

67. Who is the author of the famous work *Asian Drama : An Enquiry into the Causes of Poverty of Nations*?
    (a) Paul Streeten (b) Irving Fisher
    (c) Gunnar Myrdal (d) Kingsley Davis

9

68. Who among the following served as Professor of Economics at Harvard?
(a) E.H. Chamberlin (b) N. Kaldor
(c) J.M. Keynes (d) A.C. Pigou

69. The Cambridge School refers to the group of English economists who came under the influence of:
(a) Alfred Marshall (b) J.M. Keynes
(c) E.H. Chamberlin (d) D.H. Robertson

70. The Modern or Neo-Keynesian Theory of Interest owes it development largely to the efforts of:
(a) J.R. Hicks (b) Gunnar Myrdal (c) B. Ohlin
(d) D.H. Robertson

71. Who wrote *Economics of Imperfect Competition*?
(a) E.H. Chamberlin (b) Joan Robinson
(c) E.A.G. Robinson (d) J.R. Hicks

72. Gunnar Myrdal was awarded Noble Prize for Economics in 1974. What is his nationality?
(a) Norwegian (b) Dutch (c) Swedish
(d) American

73. Who stated explicitly for the first time the Law of Comparative Costs in the context of the theory of international trade?
(a) David Ricardo (b) Alfred Marshall
(c) F.W. Taussig (d) A.C. Pigou

74. With which of the following concepts is the name of J.M. Keynes particularly associated?
(a) Marginal propensity to save (b) Marginal propensity to consume (c) Liquidity preference
(d) All of the above

75. Identify the author of *The Affluent Society*:
(a) J.K. Galbraith (b) Gunnar Myrdal (c) John Strachey (d) N. Kaldor

76. Who wrote *A Contribution to the Theory of Trade Cycle*?
    (a)   N.   Kaldor   (b)   J.R.   Hicks
    (c) J.S. Duesenberry (d) A.H. Hansen

77. Which is the work of R.F. Harrod?
    (a) *Towards a Dynamic Economics* (b) *The Trade Cycle: An Essay* (c) *Reforming the World's Money* (d) *The Gold Standard in Theory and Practice*

78. Who among the following Noble Prize winners is an American economist?
    (a)   Richard   Stone   (b)   Ragnar   Frisch
    (c) Lawerence Klein (d) James E. Meade

79. *The General Theory of Employment, Interest and Money* is the major work of:
    (a)   N.   Kaldor   (b)   Alfred   Marshall
    (c) F.A. Hayek (d) J.M. Keynes

80. At which university was W.W. Leontief appointed Professor of Economics in 1946?
    (a) London School of Economics (b) University of Chicago (c) Harvard University (d) University of Kiel

81. Who among the following economists is not a Noble Prize winner?
    (a) Paul A. Samuelson (b) Simon Kuznets
    (c) Robert M. Solow (d) Joan Robinson

82. Which of the following is not the work of Paul A. Samuelson?
    (a) *Foundation of Economic Analysis* (b) *History of Economic Analysis* (c) *Readings in Economics* (d) *Linear Programming and Economic Analysis*

83. In which year was Paul A. Samuelson awarded the Nobel Prize for Economics?
    (a) 1970 (b) 1968 (c) 1966 (d) 1964

84. Identify the economist who first developed the Theory of Income Determination in its modern form:
(a) Paul A. Samuelson (b) J.M. Keynes (c) Joan Robinson (d) J.K. Galbraith

85. How many economists were awarded the Nobel Prize for Economics in 1990?
(a) One (b) Two (c) Three (d) Four

II
GLIMPSES OF WORLD ECONOMY

86. The overall rate of growth of global output was estimated to be 4% in 1988 and 3% in 1989. What was the estimated growth rate in 1990?
(a) 4% (b) 3% (c) 2% (d) 1%

87. The estimated average annual growth rate of GDP in high-income economics stood at 3.6% during 1989. What was this growth rate in respect of East Asia?
(a) 5.1% (b) 4.8% (c) 4.2% (d) 3.4%

88. Which country has the highest GDP in the world?
(a) Japan (b) USA (c) USSR (d) China

89. Which country in the world has the lowest GNP per capita?
(a) Mozambique (b) Ethiopia (c) Chad (d) Tanzania

90. Which country in the world has the highest per capita income?
(a) USA (b) Switzerland (c) Japan (d) Sweden

91. Identify the region where it is expected that the number of poor will increase between 1985 and 2000:

(a) East Asia (b) Sub-Saharan Africa (c) South Asia (d) Eastern Europe

92. Identify the country where the share of agriculture in the gross domestic product is highest:
(a) Tanzania (b) Uganda (c) Nepal (d) Somalia

93. Indonesia took less than a generation in the 1970s and 1980s to reduce the incidence of poverty from almost 60% to less than:
(a) 30% (b) 25% (c) 20% (d) 15%

94. South Asia accounts for roughly 30% of the world's population. What percentage of the world's poor lives in this region?
(a) 56 (b) 52 (c) 46 (d) 40

95. The number of people living in poverty in East Asia stood at around 280 million in 1985. By the end of the present century this number is projected to fall sharply to:
(a) 110 million (b) 90 million (c) 70 million (d) 50 million

96. The developing countries witnessed a growth rate of 4.3% in GDP during 1980-89. Which of the following regions recorded the highest rate of growth at 8.4% during this period?
(a) South Asia (b) East Asia (c) Eastern Europe (d) Latin America and the Caribbean

97. What is the present percentage contribution of agriculture in the United States to the country's gross domestic product?
(a) 1 (b) 2 (c) 3 (d) 4

98. Which low-income country leads in fertiliser consumption per hectare of arable land?
(a) Sri Lanka (b) Indonesia (c) Pakistan (d) China

99. The contribution of industry in China to the country's gross domestic product stood at 39% in 1965. What was this percentage in 1988?
(a) 42 (b) 44 (c) 46 (d) 48

100. In which country is the contribution of services to gross domestic product highest at around 73%?
(a) Jordan (b) USA (c) Hong Kong (d) Panama

101. The share of agriculture in the gross domestic product of Japan declined from 9% in 1965 to . . . . in 1988:
(a) 3% (b) 4% (c) 5% (d) 6%

102. According to the World Development Report 1990, low-income economies were those with a GNP per capita of $ . . . . or less in 1988:
(a) 525 (b) 545 (c) 575 (d) 600

103. The number of poor in the developing world is projected to fall from 1125 million in 1985 to about . . . . million by the end of the present century:
(a) 950 (b) 900 (c) 850 (d) 825

104. Identify the country which has the largest per capita daily calorie intake:
(a) Denmark (b) USA (c) United Arab Emirates (d) Greece

105. Gross national savings during 1980-88, as a percentage of gross national product, was highest in:
(a) Yugoslavia (b) Algeria (c) Portugal (d) Malaysia

106. The rate of gross domestic savings in China was 25% in 1965. What was this rate in 1988?
(a) 37% (b) 33% (c) 30% (d) 28%

107. Which is the most heavily indebted country in the world today?
(a) India (b) Brazil (c) Mexico (d) Argentina

108. Which country in the world has made the largest use of IMF credit?
(a) Mexico (b) Argentina (c) India (d) China

109. Identify the country which leads in terms of per capita aid receipts:
(a) Israel (b) Jordan (c) Zambia (d) Senegal

110. Identify the country which showed the highest average annual inflation during 1980-88:
(a) Uganda (b) Bolivia (c) Peru (d) Argentina

111. In which high-income country is the per capita energy consumption generally found to be highest?
(a) USA (b) Norway (c) Canada (d) Sweden

112. Which country, among the low-income countries, occupies the first place in respect of per capita energy consumption?
(a) China (b) India (c) Indonesia (d) Yemen

113. Where was the average annual growth rate of energy production highest during the eighties?
(a) Thailand (b) Denmark (c) Malaysia (d) Cameroon

114. As against real export growth of 4.8% in industrial countries during 1980-89, the developing countries recorded a growth rate of about:
(a) 4.5% (b) 5.0% (c) 5.5% (d) 6.0%

115. Identify the rate of growth in the volume of world exports during 1990:
(a) 7.0% (b) 6.5% (c) 6.0% (d) 5.5%

116. Which of the following countries has the largest population?

(a) Japan (b) Brazil (c) Bangladesh (d) Indonesia

117. The urban population in the Soviet Union was 52% of the country's population in 1965. What was this percentage in 1988?
(a) 60 (b) 62 (c) 65 (d) 67

118. The present life expectancy at birth in the USSR is estimated to be:
(a) 72 (b) 70 (c) 68 (d) 66

119. The total population of China in AD 2000 is projected to be:
(a) 1000 million (b) 1080 million (c) 1180 million (d) 1280 million

120. What is the birth rate per thousand in the Soviet Union?
(a) 22 (b) 20 (c) 18 (d) 16

121. Identify the low-income country where life expectancy at birth for females is highest:
(a) China (b) Sri Lanka (c) Indonesia (d) Kenya

122. In which country in the world is the Central Government expenditure on health, as a percentage of its total expenditure, highest?
(a) Costa Rica (b) USA (c) Germany (d) UK

123. Among the low-income countries, the Central Government expenditure on education as a percentage of its total expenditure, is highest in:
(a) Kenya (b) Togo (c) Ethiopia (d) Ghana

124. There is one particular country where the entire population is urban in character. Identify the country:
(a) Singapore (b) Belgium (c) Kuwait (d) Hong Kong

125. Among low-income countries, the crude birth rate is highest in:
(a) Malawi (b) Rwanda (c) Uganda (d) Zambia

126. The percentage of married women of child-bearing age using contraception is highest at 78 in two countries. One is the Federal Republic of Germany. Which is the other?
(a) USA (b) France (c) Mauritus (d) Canada

127. Sri Lanka has the lowest death rate among low-income countries. What is its death rate per 1000 persons?
(a) 9 (b) 8 (c) 7 (d) 6

128. Which country in the world has the lowest death rate?
(a) Japan (b) Canada (c) Hong Kong (d) Kuwait

129. China has made rapid progress in the sphere of family planning. What is the percentage of married women of child-bearing age using contraception in China?
(a) 76 (b) 74 (c) 68 (d) 60

130. The crude birth rate per thousand population is highest in Malawi. Identify the birth rate:
(a) 54 (b) 52 (c) 50 (d) 48

131. The crude birth rate per thousand population in France stood at 18 in 1965. What was this rate in 1988?
(a) 16 (b) 15 (c) 14 (d) 13

132. Which developed country has the highest infant mortality rate?
(a) USA (b) UK (c) Sweden (d) USSR

133. The under five mortality rate in the developing world stood at 102 per thousand during 1985-90. In which of the following regions was it found to be the lowest at 25 per thousand?

(a) East Asia (b) Eastern Europe (c) South Asia
(d) Middle East and North Africa

134. Which country has the largest number of cities of over five lakh persons?
(a) USA (b) China (c) India (d) Australia

135. Which low-income country is expected to reach the net reproductive rate of 1 at the earliest?
(a) Sri Lanka (b) China (c) India (d) Pakistan

136. The percentage of population in the age-group 15-64 is highest in:
(a) China (b) Japan (c) Singapore
(d) Hong Kong

137. In which low-income country is the highest adult illiteracy to be found?
(a) Chad (b) Niger (c) Mali (d) Somalia

138. Which high-income country is characterised by highest adult illiteracy?
(a) Singapore (b) Spain (c) Hong Kong
(d) Kuwait

139. Sub-Saharan Africa recorded the highest average annual population growth rate during 1980-90. Identify the growth rate:
(a) 2.3% (b) 2.7% (c) 2.9% (d) 3.2%

140. Japan has the highest life expectancy at birth in the world at:
(a) 70 years (b) 72 years (c) 74 years (d) 76 years

141. Which country has the lowest life expectancy at birth?
(a) Sierra Leone (b) Guinea (c) Niger
(d) Malawi

142. Of the following four countries, which country has comparatively larger area?

(a) France (b) Sweden (c) Spain (d) New Zealand

143. In 1989 food aid to developing countries amounted to approximately . . . . billion dollars:
(a) 1.5 (b) 2.0 (c) 2.5 (d) 3.2

144. Which is the biggest source of aid to the Third World?
(a) The World Bank (b) USA (c) Japan (d) International Development Association

145. Which country ranks first in the world in milk production?
(a) USA (b) USSR (c) India (d) Australia

146. Which country has the world's largest cattle population?
(a) Australia (b) USA (c) China (d) India

147. German cars are exported in largest numbers to:
(a) USA (b) UK (b) Canada (d) France

148. When was the world's first set of traveller's cheques issued by the American Express Company?
(a) 1861 (b) 1871 (c) 1881 (d) 1891

149. Which country was the world's largest donor in 1989?
(a) Japan (b) USA (c) USSR (d) UK

150. Approximately what percentage of the world's total oil-reserves are found in West Asia?
(a) 70 (b) 65 (c) 60 (d) 55

151. The Soviet Union has about 5.8% of the world's oil reserves. What is its share in the world output of oil?
(a) 8% (b) 12% (c) 16% (d) 20%

152. Since what date in August 1990 did the US dollar and other currencies become convertible for Soviet citizens?
(a) First (b) Fifth (c) Tenth (d) Fifteenth

153. On what day in October 1990 did the Soviet Parliament approve Gorbachov's market economy plan?
(a) Fifteenth (b) Seventeenth (d) Nineteenth (d) Twenty-first

154. On what day in October 1990 did the unification of East Germany and West Germany take place?
(a) First (b) Third (c) Fifth (d) Seventh

155. Which day is observed as the World Food Day?
(a) 20 September (b) 16 October (d) 4 November (d) 15 December

156. Identify the terminal year of the First Five-year Plan of China:
(a) 1958 (b) 1957 (d) 1956 (d) 1955

157. Compared to the average annual growth rate of GNP per capita at 1.8% in India during 1965-88, the growth rate in China was:
(a) 2.6% (b) 3.2% (c) 4.6% (d) 5.4%

158. What was the average annual growth rate of GNP per capita in Japan during 1965-88?
(a) 4.3% (b) 3.5% (c) 3.1% (d) 2.9%

159. What is roughly the percentage contribution of industry to Japan's gross domestic product?
(a) 55 (b) 47 (c) 45 (d) 41

160. How many five-year plans had been completed in the Soviet Union by 1980?
(a) Twelve (b) Eleven (c) Ten (d) Nine

161. What was the average annual growth rate during the first decade of planning in the Soviet Union?

(a) 15.8% (b) 13.4% (c) 10.2% (d) 8.6%

162. In which month of 1917 did the Bolshevik Revolution take place in the Soviet Union?
(a) September (b) October (c) November (d) December

163. The Great Britain received loans amounting to .... between 1948 and 1950 under the U.S. Marshall Plan for its recovery programme:
(a) £ 1500 million (b) £ 1200 million (c) £ 1100 million (d) £ 1000 million

164. Which is not an essential characteristic feature of French Planning?
(a) Indicative Planning (b) Flexible Planning (c) Corporative Planning (d) Centralised Planning

165. The Sixth Plan of France covered the period:
(a) 1976-80 (b) 1971-75 (c) 1968-72 (d) 1966-70

166. The US Government, under President Roosevelt, began in 1933 a number of projects designed to stimulate recovery from the Great Depression. These came to be termed as:
(a) New Deal (b) New Economic Policy (c) Recovery Plan (d) Roosevelt Programme

167. In which country did the Industrial Revolution first occur?
(a) France (b) United States (c) Germany (d) England

168. When was the Sherman Anti-Trust Act in the United States passed?
(a) 1914 (d) 1901 (d) 1898 (d) 1890

III

INTERNATIONAL ECONOMIC ORGANISATIONS

169. When did the International Monetary Fund (IMF) begin its operations?
(a) 1945 (b) 1946 (c) 1947 (d) 1948

170. What is the present total number of members of the IMF?
(a) 135 (b) 142 (c) 148 (d) 155

172. Where are the headquarters of the IMF?
(a) Paris (b) Geneva (c) New York (d) Washington, DC

172. What rate of interest does the IMF charge for providing additional concessional balance of payments assistance, under the structural adjustment facility, to low-income countries?
(a) 2% (b) 1.5% (c) 1% (d) 0.5%

173. When was the first amendment to the Articles of the IMF made which led to the creation of the Special Drawing Rights (SDR) facility?
(a) 1969 (b) 1971 (c) 1975 (d) 1978

174. Which one of the following is not a function of the IMF?
(a) To promote international monetary co-operation (b) To promote exchange stability (c) To promote a multilateral trading system (d) To promote the development of backward countries

175. The IMF Institute conducts courses, covering a wide spectrum of subjects in financial analysis and policy-making, for officials from member-

countries in Washington. When was it established?

(a) 1962 (b) 1964 (c) 1966 (d) 1968

176. The IMF approves the creation of a given amount of new SDRs. These SDRs are distributed among the participating countries on the basis of their:

(a) Needs (b) Share in world trade (c) Quotas in the IMF (d) Balance of payments deficits

177. Which of the following currencies is at present not included in the valuation of the SDRs?

(a) Pound sterling (b) Yen (c) Mark (d) Dinar

178. In 1974 the IMF changed the basis of valuation of the SDR by calculating the value of the SDR from a basket of currencies of several major countries. What was the number of currencies included in the valuation of the SDR in 1974?

(a) 16 (b) 14 (c) 12 (d) 10

177. Where are the headquarters of the International Labour Organisation (ILO)?

(a) Rome (b) Geneva (c) London (d) New York

180. When was the ILO established as an autonomous part of the League of Nations?

(a) 1918 (b) 1919 (c) 1920 (d) 1921

181. In which year was the ILO awarded the Nobel Peace Prize?

(a) 1965 (b) 1969 (c) 1973 (d) 1977

182. Which is the oldest organisation among the four?

(a) ILO (b) FAO (c) WHO (d) IMF

183. What was the total number of member-countries of the Colombo Plan for Co-operative Economic Development in South and South-East Asia which was set up in 1950?

(a) Seven (b) Fifteen (c) Twenty (d) Twenty-six

184. One of the following countries was not a member country of the Colombo Plan. Identify it:
(a) India (b) Iran (c) USA (d) France

185. In which month of 1945 was the Food and Agriculture Organisation (FAO) set up?
(a) August (b) September (c) October (d) November

186. In 1951 the FAO was transferred from its temporary headquarters in Washington, DC to:
(a) Rome (b) New York (c) Ottawa (d) Geneva

187. The FAO come into formal being in 1945 with the signing of its constitution at a conference held in:
(a) Washington, DC (b) Virginia (c) Quebec City (d) New York

188. An affiliate of the World Bank, the International Finance Corporation (IFC) became effective in:
(a) 1956 (b) 1960 (c) 1962 (d) 1964

189. The International Bank for Reconstruction and Development (IBRD), known as World Bank, began its operations in:
(a) 1944 (b) 1945 (c) 1946 (d) 1947

190. The main function of the World Bank is to:
(a) Encourage capital investment for the reconstruction and development of its member-countries (b) Grant long-term loans at little or no interest for projects in developing countries (c) Reduce trade barriers and establish rules of free trade (d) Facilitate poor countries to trade at concessional rates

191. At what rate of interest does the World Bank provide loan to underdeveloped countries?
(a) 7.5% (b) 6.5% (c) 5.5% (d) 4.5%

192. The highest percentage of the World Bank's total loans have been made for the development of:
(a) Industry (b) Agriculture (c) Energy (d) Transport

193. The World Bank normally gives:
(a) Short-term loans (b) Medium-term loans (c) Long-term loans (d) Medium and long-term loans

194. In which of the following ways does the World Bank give loans to members?
(a) By granting or participating in direct loans out of its own funds (b) By granting loans out of funds raised in the market (c) By guaranteeing loans made by private investors through investment channels (d) All of the above

195. How many governments have contributed to the capital of the World Bank?
(a) 144 (b) 150 (c) 154 (d) 158

196. An affiliate of the World Bank, the International Development Association (IDA) was set up in:
(a) 1950 (b) 1956 (c) 1960 (d) 1962

197. Where are the headquarters of the IDA?
(a) Washington, DC (b) London (c) Geneva (d) New York

198. The IDA gives development credits to the developing countries for a period of at least:
(a) 10 years (b) 15 years (c) 20 years (d) 25 years

199. How many lending nations formed the 'Aid India Club' to help India out of her foreign exchange difficulties?
(a) 14 (b) 12 (c) 10 (d) 8

200. Which of the following does not match?
(a) Food and Agricultural Organisation — Rome (b) International Monetary Fund — Washington, DC (c) United Nations Fund for Population Activities — New York (d) International Fund for Agricultural Development — Geneva

201. The main function of the IFC is to:
(a) Make special efforts to promote international trade (b) Encourage the growth of productive private enterprises in less developed member countries (c) Assist those countries with an annual per capita gross national product of less than $520 (d) Promote foreign investment

202. Which financial institution is known as the 'soft loan window' from which underdeveloped countries can borrow in hard currencies?
(a) IBRD (b) IFC (c) IDA (d) IMF

203. The main function of the IDA is to:
(a) Achieve international co-operation in the field of economics (b) Make loans to less developed countries on flexible terms (c) Stabilise exchange rates (d) Promote foreign private investment by guarantees

204. An international conference was held in Geneva in 1947 to consider matters relating to common trade and tariff policy which led to the establishment of the General Agreement on Tariffs and Trade (GATT) in the following

year. How many countries attended this conference?
(a) 19 (b) 21 (c) 23 (d) 25

205. Where are the headquarters of the General Agreement on Tariffs and Trade (GATT) organisation?
(a) Geneva (b) Washington, DC (c) London (d) Ottawa

206. There have been a series of rounds of negotiations between the signatories of GATT designed to reduce trade barriers on a multilateral basis. The first round tooks place in 1947. Which round came to be known as Kennedy Round?
(a) Third (b) Fourth (c) Fifth (d) Sixth

207. When was the Uruguay Round of multilateral trade negotiations under the GATT launched?
(a) January 1986 (b) June 1986 (c) September 1986 (d) December 1986

208. Including the Uruguay Round, how many multilateral trade negotiations have been held in the GATT so far?
(a) Nine (b) Eight (c) Seven (d) Six

209. The headquarters of the World Health Organisation are located at:
(a) Paris (b) London (c) Geneva (c) New York

210. When was the World Health Organisation (WHO) set up?
(a) 1945 (b) 1946 (c) 1947 (d) 1948

211. Where are the headquarters of the United Nations Fund for Population Activities located?
(a) Geneva (b) New York (c) London (d) Paris

212. When was the United Nations Fund for Population Activities set up?
(a) 1967 (b) 1969 (c) 1971 (d) 1973

213. Where is the central secretariat of the Association of South-East Asian Nations (ASEAN) located?
(a) Jakarta (b) Kuala Lampur (c) Manila (d) Bangkok

214. The aim of the ASEAN is to accelerate economic and social progress and maintain stability in the region. When was it formed?
(a) 1965 (b) 1966 (c) 1967 (d) 1968

215. How many countries are members of the ASEAN?
(a) Five (b) Six (c) Seven (d) Eight

216. The International Fund for Agricultural Development is a one billion dollar fund used for raising food production in developing countries and providing employment to poor and landless farmers. What proportion of this fund has been contributed by industrialised nations?
(a) 40% (b) 50% (c) 60% (d) 70%

217. When was the International Fund for Agricultural Development set up?
(a) 1977 (b) 1975 (c) 1973 (d) 1971

218. The International Fund for Agricultural Development has its headquarters in:
(a) London (b) Rome (c) Geneva (d) New York

219. When was the Council of Europe, which aims to protect and promote economic and social progress of its members, set up?
(a) 1948 (b) 1949 (c) 1950 (d) 1951

220. Where are the headquarters of the Council of Europe?
(a) Vienna (b) Strasbourg (c) Bonn (d) Luxembourg

221. Two organisations were conceived at the Bretton Woods conference held in 1944. One was the IBRD. Which was the other?
(a) FAO (b) GATT (c) IMF (d) IDA

222. Where are the headquarters of the United Nations Industrial Development Organisation (UNIDO)?
(a) Vienna (b) Geneva (c) Ottawa (d) Washington, DC

223. When was the Organisation of Economic Co-operation and Development (OECD) formed?
(a) 1948 (b) 1953 (c) 1958 (d) 1961

224. The headquarters of OECD are located at:
(a) Paris (b) Vienna (c) Brussels (d) New York

225. Where are the headquarters of the European Economic Community?
(a) Paris (b) Brussels (c) Copenhagen (d) London

226. How many countries are the members of the European Economic Community (EEC)?
(a) 12 (b) 10 (c) 8 (d) 6

227. Identify one of the new members of the European Economic Community?
(a) Spain (b) France (c) Great Britain (d) Denmark

228. In which year did the European Economic Community (EEC), popularly known as the European Common Market (ECM), come into existence?
(a) 1956 (b) 1958 (c) 1960 (d) 1962

229. Which one of the following countries attends the sessions of the Council for Mutual Economic Assistance as an observer?
(a) Poland (b) Mexico (c) Peru (d) Romania

230. The headquarters of the Council for Mutual Economic Assistance (COMECON) are located at:
(a) Moscow (b) Havana (c) Warsaw (d) Budapest

231. When was the Council for Mutual Economic Assistance (COMECON) founded with the object of co-ordinating and integrating the economies of member-countries?
(a) 1948 (b) 1949 (c) 1950 (d) 1951

232. How many countries joined together to form the European Free Trade Association (EFTA) with a view to ultimately establish a free trade area between member-countries?
(a) Six (b) Seven (c) Eight (d) Nine

233. Two founder members of the European Free Trade Association (EFTA) left it in 1972 to join the EEC. One was the UK. Which was the other?
(a) Norway (b) Sweden (c) Denmark (d) Portugal

234. Where are the headquarters of EFTA located?
(a) Geneva (b) Brussels (c) Stockholm (d) Vienna

235. The European Free Trade Association (EFTA) was formed on the pattern of the EEC as a result of the convention signed by some countries of Europe at Stockholm. When was it formed?
(a) 1959 (b) 1960 (c) 1961 (d) 1962

236. When was the United Nations Environment Programme launched?
(a) 1970 (b) 1971 (c) 1972 (d) 1973

237. Which of the following organisations has its headquarters at Nairobi?

(a) United Nations Development Programme
(b) United Nations Environment Programme
(c) Organisation of African Unity (d) Universal
Postal Union

238. When was the 'Group of 77', an economic
group of the Third World countries to protect
the economic and trade interests of developing
countries, formed under the auspices of the
United Nations?
(a) 1962 (b) 1964 (c) 1966 (d) 1968

239. When was the World Bank's Special Programme of Assistance (SPA) for indebted low-
income countries initiated?
(a) December 1987 (b) January 1988
(c) March 1988 (d) May 1988

240. Which country is the OPEC's largest oil exporter?
(a) Saudi Arabia (b) Iraq (c) Kuwait (d) United
Arab Emirates

241. When was the Organisation of Petroleum Ex-
porting Countries (OPEC) formed to control
the production and pricing of crude oil?
(a) 1956 (b) 1958 (c) 1960 (d) 1962

242. The headquarters of which of the following
organisations are located at Vienna?
(a) OPEC (b) COMECON (c) OECD (d) IDA

243. The International Air Transport Association
(IATA) aims to promote safe, regular and
economical air transport and to provide a
forum for collaboration. When was its
founded?
(a) 1945 (b) 1946 (c) 1947 (d) 1948

244. How many international airlines are active
members of the IATA?
(a) 35 (b) 40 (c) 45 (d) 50

245. Which of the following is not a member-country of the G-7 (Group of Seven advanced industrial nations)?
(a) USA (b) UK (c) USSR (d) Italy

246. Which of the following organisations was brought into existence by the Treaty of Rome?
(a) Council for Mutual Economic Assistance
(b) European Free Trade Association
(c) European Economic Community
(d) Council of Europe

247. How many Regional Economic Commissions have been set up by the United Nations Economic and Social Council?
(a) Eight (b) Seven (c) Six (d) Five

248. How many member-states are represented in the United Nations Economic and Social Council?
(a) 44 (b) 50 (c) 54 (d) 58

249. In which year was the Asian Development Bank (ADB) set up following the recommendation of the United Nations Economic Commission for Asia and Far East?
(a) 1964 (b) 1966 (c) 1968 (d) 1970

250. When was the Asian Development Fund launched by the Asian Development Bank with a view to provide concessional credit to needy members?
(a) 1974 (b) 1972 (c) 1970 (d) 1968

IV

DEMAND, SUPPLY AND PRICE

251. Economic problems arise because:
(a) Wants are unlimited (b) Resources are scarce (c) Scarce resources have alternative uses (d) All of the above

252. Which is not an essential condition for an economic problem to arise?
(a) Unlimited wants (b) Use of money (c) Scarcity of resources (d) Alternative uses of scarce resources

253. Which is not a central problem of an economy?
(a) What to produce (b) How to produce (c) How to maximise private profit (d) For whom to produce

254. Who defined Economics as a 'Science which studies human behaviour as a relationship between ends and means which have alternative uses'?
(a) L. Robbins (b) Alfred Marshall (c) Joan Robinson (d) Paul A. Samuelson

255. A mixed economy is characterised by the co-existence of:
(a) Modern and traditional industries (b) Public and private sectors (c) Foreign and domestic investments (d) Commercial and subsistence farming

256. Which is not an essential feature of a socialist economy?
(a) Social ownership of the means of production (b) Freedom of enterprise (c) Use of centralised planning (d) Government decisions

257. Which of the following is incorrect?
(a) A function shows the relationship between two or more variables (b) Normative Economics studies how the economic problems facing society should be solved (c) A market necessarily refers to a meeting place between buyers and sellers (d) Equilibrium refers to the market conditions which once achieved, tend to persist

258. Microeconomics deals with the:
(a) Allocation of resources of the economy as between production of different goods and services (b) Determination of prices of goods and services (c) Behaviour of industrial decision-makers (d) All of the above

259. Which of the following is Microeconomics concerned with?
(a) The size of national output (b) The level of employment (c) Changes in the general level of prices (d) None of the above

260. Formulation of an economic theory involves:
(a) Statement of various assumptions or postulates (b) Logical deductions from the assumptions made (c) Testing the hypotheses against empirical evidence (d) All of the above

261. An economic theory is:
(a) An axiom (b) A proposition (c) A hypothesis (d) A tested hypothesis

262. Identify the aspect of taxation which is related to normative economics:
(a) Incidence of tax (b) Effect of tax on the capacity/willingness to work (c) Equity of tax (d) None of the above

263. Demand for a commodity refers to a:

(a) Desire for the commodity (b) Need for the commodity (c) Quantity demanded of that commodity (d) Quantity of the commodity demanded at a certain price during any particular period of time.

264. Contraction of demand is the result of:
(a) Decrease in the number of consumers (b) Increase in the price of the commodity concerned (c) Increase in the prices of other goods (d) Decrease in the income of purchasers

265. All but one of the following are assumed to remain the same while drawing an individual's demand curve for a commodity. Which one is it?
(a) The preferences of the individual (b) His monetary income (c) The price of the commodity under consideration (d) The prices of other goods

266. Which of the following pairs of commodities is an example of substitutes?
(a) Tea and sugar (b) Tea and coffee (c) Pen and ink (d) Shirt and trousers

267. In the case of a straight line demand curve meeting the two axes, the price-elasticity of demand at the mid-point of the line would be:
(a) 0 (b) 1 (c) 1.5 (d) 2

268. The Law of Demand, assuming other things to remain constant, establishes the relationship between:
(a) Income of the consumer and the quantity of a commodity demanded by him (b) Price of a commodity and the quantity demanded (c) Price of a commodity and the demand for its substitute (d) Quantity demanded of a

commodity and the relative prices of its complementary goods

269. Identify the factor which generally keeps the price-elasticity of demand for a commodity low:
(a) Variety of uses for that commodity (b) Its low price (c) Close substitutes for that commodity (d) High proportion of the consumer's income spent on it

270. Identify the coefficient of price-elasticity of demand when the percentage increase in the quantity of a commodity demanded is smaller than the percentage fall in its price:
(a) Equal to one (b) Greater than one (c) Smaller than one (d) Zero

271. In the case of an inferior good, the income elasticity of demand is:
(a) Positive (b) Zero (c) Negative (d) Infinite

272. In respect of which of the following category of goods is consumer's surplus highest?
(a) Giffen goods (b) Necessities (c) Luxuries (d) Prestige goods

273. Total utility is maximum when:
(a) Marginal utility is zero (b) Marginal utility is at its highest point (c) Marginal utility is equal to average (d) Average utility is maximum

274. If the demand for a commodity is inelastic, an increase in its price will cause the total expenditure of the consumers of the commodity to:
(a) Remain the same (b) Increase (c) Decrease (d) Any of the above

275. If regardless of changes in its price, the quantity demanded of a commodity remains

unchanged, then the demand curve for the commodity will be:
(a) Horizontal (b) Vertical (c) Positively sloped (d) Negatively sloped

276. In the case of a Giffen good, the demand curve will be:
(a) Horizontal (b) Downward-sloping to the right (c) Backward falling to the left (d) Upward-sloping to the right

277. The budget-line is also known as the:
(a) Iso-utility curve (b) Production possibility line (c) Isoquant (d) Consumption possibility line

278. Which one is not a assumption of the theory of demand based on analysis of indifference curves?
(a) Given scale of preferences as between different combinations of two goods (b) Diminishing marginal rate of substitution (c) Constant marginal utility of money (d) Consumers would always prefer more of a particular good to less of it, other things remaining the same

279. The elasticity of substitution between two perfect substitutions is:
(a) Zero (b) Greater than zero (c) Less than infinity (d) infinity

280. The consumer is in equilibrium at a point where the budget line:
(a) Is above an indifference curve (b) Is below an indifference curve (c) Is tangent to an indifference curve (d) Cuts an indifference curve

281. An indifference curve slopes down towards right since more of one commodity and less of another result in:

37

(a) Same satisfaction (b) Greater satisfaction (c) Maximum satisfaction (d) Decreasing expenditure

282. The Revealed Preference Theory deduces the inverse price-quantity relationship from:
(a) Assumption of indifference (b) Postulate of utility maximization (c) Observed behaviour of the consumer (d) Introspection

283. Which of the following statements is incorrect?
(a) An indifference curve must be downward-sloping to the right (b) Convexity of a curve implies that the slope of the curve diminishes as one moves from left to right (c) The elasticity of substitution between two goods to a consumer is zero (d) The total effect of a change in the price of a good on its quantity demanded is called the price effect

284. Production is a function of:
(a) Profits (b) Costs (c) Inputs (d) Price

285. An iso-product curve slopes:
(a) Downward to the left (b) Downward to the right (c) Upward to the left (d) Upward to the right

286. A vertical supply curve parallel to the price-axis implies that the elasticity of supply is:
(a) Zero (b) Infinity (c) Equal to one (d) Greater than zero but less than infinity

287. The supply of a commodity refers to:
(a) Actual production of the commodity (b) Total existing stock of the commodity (c) Stock available for sale (d) Amount of the commodity offered for sale at a particular price per unit of time

288. Which cost increases continuously with the increase in production?

(a) Average cost (b) Marginal cost (c) Fixed cost (d) Variable cost

289. Which of the following cost curves is never U-shaped?
(a) Average cost curve (b) Marginal cost curve (c) Average variable cost curve (d) Average fixed cost curve

290. Total costs in the short-term are classified into fixed costs and variable costs. Which one of the following is a variable cost?
(a) Cost of raw materials (b) Cost of equipment (c) Interest payment on past borrowing (d) Payment of rent on buildings

291. In the short term, when the output of a firm increases, its average fixed cost:
(a) Increase (b) Decrease (c) Remains constant (d) First declines and then rises

292. A significant property of the Cobb—Douglas production function is that the elasticity of substitution between inputs is:
(a) Equal to unity (b) More than unity (c) Less than unity (d) Zero

293. The production techniques are technically efficient:
(a) Below the lower ridge line (b) Above the upper ridge line (c) Between the two ridge lines (d) On the upper ridge line

294. Which of the following is not a feature of iso-product curves? Iso-product curves:
(a) Are downward sloping to the right (b) Show different input combination producing the same output (c) Intersect each other (d) Are convex to the origin

295. Some economists refer to iso-product curves as:

(a) Engel's curve (b) Production indifference curve (c) Budget line (d) Ridge line

296. Which one of the following is also known as plant curves?
(a) Long-run average cost (LAC) curves
(b) Short-run average cost (SAC) curves
(c) Average variable cost (AVC) curves
(d) Average total cost (ATC) curves

297. What is the shape of the average fixed cost (AFC) curve?
(a) U-shape (b) Horizontal upto a point and then rising (c) Sloping down towards the right (d) Rectangular hyperbola

298. An increase in the supply of a commodity is caused by:
(a) Improvements in its technology (b) Fall in the prices of other commodities (c) Fall in the prices of factors of production (d) All of the above

299. Elasticity of supply refers to the degree of responsiveness of supply of a commodity to changes in its:
(a) Demand (b) Price (c) Costs of production (d) State of technology

300. The cost of one thing in terms of the alternative given up is known as:
(a) Production cost (b) Physical cost (c) Real cost (d) Opportunity cost

301. According to current thinking, the law of diminishing returns applies to:
(a) All fields of production (b) Agriculture (c) Mining (d) Manufacturing

302. Identify the correct statement:
(a) The average product is at its maximum when the marginal product is equal to the

average product (b) The law of increasing returns relates to the effect of changes in factor proportions (c) Economies of scale arise only because of indivisibilities of factors of production (d) The production possibility curve and the transformation curve are different curves

303. With which of the following is the concept of marginal cost closely related?
(a) Variable cost (b) Fixed cost (c) Implicit cost (d) Explicit cost

304. According to M. Kalecki, the true measure of the degree of monopoly power is the:
(a) Ratio between price and marginal cost (b) Extent of monopolistic profit enjoyed by the monopolist (c) Cross-elasticity of demand for the product of the monopolist (d) Price charged by the monopolist minus marginal cost of production

305. A monopolist is able to maximise his profit when:
(a) His output is maximum (b) He charges a high price (c) His average cost is minimum (d) His marginal revenue is equal to marginal cost

306. Which of the following is not an essential condition of pure competition?
(a) Large number of buyers and sellers (b) Homogeneous product (c) Freedom of entry (d) Absence of transport cost

307. What is the shape of the demand curve faced by a firm under perfect competition?
(a) Horizontal (b) Vertical (c) Positively sloped (d) Negatively sloped

308. Which is the first-order condition for the profit of a firm to be maximum?

(a) AC = MR (b) MC = MR (c) MR = AR
(d) AC = AR

309. In which form of the market structure in the degree of control over the price of its product by a firm very large?
(a) Monopoly (b) Imperfect competition
(c) Oligopoly (d) Perfect competition

310. Which is the other name that is given to the average revenue curve?
(a) Profit curve (b) Demand curve (c) Average cost curve (d) Indifference curve

311. Under which of the following forms of market structure does a firm have no control over the price of its product?
(a) Monopoly (b) Monopolistic competition
(c) Oligopoly (d) Perfect competition

312. Which one of the following is the condition of equilibrium for the monopolist?
(a) MR = MC (b) MC = AR (c) MR = MC = Price (d) AC = AR

313. The situation of monopolistic competition is created by:
(a) Small number of producers of a commodity
(b) Lack of homogeneity of the product produced by different firms (c) Imperfection of the market for that product (d) All of the above

314. Discriminating monopoly implies that the monopolist charges different prices for his commodity:
(a) From different groups of consumers
(b) For different uses (c) At different places
(d) Any of the above

315. Price discrimination will be profitable only if the elasticity of demand in different markets

into which the total market has been divided is:

(a) Uniform (b) Different (c) Less (d) Zero

316. Which of the following oligopoly models is concerned with the maximisation of joint profits?

(a) Price leadership model (b) Bertrand's model (c) Collusive model (d) Edgeworth's model

317. The Kinky demand curve hypothesis is designed to explain in the context of oligopoly:

(a) Price and output determination (b) Price rigidity (c) Price leadership (d) Collusion among rivals

318. Which form of market structure is characterised by interdependence in decision-making as between the different competing firms?

(a) Oligopoly (b) Perfect competition (c) Imperfect competition (d) None of the above

319. Which one of the following is not the assumption of the Marginal Productivity Theory of Distribution?

(a) Homogeneity of a factor (b) Perfect competition in the factor market (c) All factors, except one, are variable (d) Given stock of each factor and full employment

320. With which of the theories of wages is the name of John Stuart Mill associated?

(a) Marginal productivity theory of wages (b) Wages-fund theory (c) Subsistence theory of wages (d) Iron law of wages

321. Under monopsony in the labour market, the supply curve of labour facing the firm will be:

(a) Upward-sloping to the right (b) Downward-sloping to the right (c) Backward-sloping to the left (d) Horizontal

322. Economic rent can accrue to:
(a) Land only (b) Capital only (c) Specialised technical personnel only (d) Any of the factors of production

323. Which of the following statements is incorrect:
(a) Quasi-rent is a purely short-term phenomenon (b) Rent is exclusively demand determined (c) Rent can accrue to land alone (d) Rent is the excess of actual earnings over transfer earnings

324. In the context of the firm as a whole, quasi-rent is defined as the excess of the total receipts over the total:
(a) Fixed cost (b) Average cost (c) Fixed and variable cost (d) Variable cost

325. A factor of production, whose supply is fixed in the short run, may get additional earnings. These earnings are generally referred to as:
(a) Surplus value (b) Quasi-rent (c) Transfer earnings (d) Supernormal profit

326. Which of the following factors forms the basis of the Loanable Funds Theory of Interest?
(a) Monetary factors (b) Psychological factors (c) Technical factors (d) Monetary and non-monetary factors

327. Which of the following purposes normally does not give rise to the demand for loanable funds?
(a) Consumption (b) Saving (c) Investment (d) Hoarding

328. On which of the following does the demand for money for speculative motive mainly depend?

(a) Income (b) Profits (c) Rate of interest (d) General price level

329. The demand for liquidity preference is governed by:
(a) Transaction motives (b) Precautionary motives (c) Speculative motives (d) All of these

330. Identify the neo-classical theory of the rate of interest:
(a) Liquidity-preference theory (b) Time-preference theory (c) Abstinence theory (d) Loanable funds theory

331. The classical theory explained interest as a reward for:
(a) Parting with liquidity (b) Abstinence (c) Saving (d) Inconvenience

332. According to Joseph Schumpeter, profit is the reward for:
(a) Innovation (b) Uncertainty-bearing (c) Risk-taking (d) Management

333. The term 'normal profit' as used in the analysis of equilibrium of the firm under perfect competition, refers to:
(a) Earnings of management (b) Reward for enterprise (c) Reward for innovation (d) Residual income of a business

334. Who argued that pure profit can arise only in a dynamic economy?
(a) F.H. Knight (b) J.B. Clark (c) Böhm Bawerk (d) Alfred Marshall

V

MONEY, BANKING AND
INTERNATIONAL TRADE

335. Which one of the following approaches to the definition of money gives the widest possible view of money?
(a) Central bank approach (b) Conventional approach (c) Chicago approach (d) Gurley-Shaw approach

336. The best example of representative full-bodied money is found in the 'gold certificates' which circulated in the U.S.A. before being withdrawn from circulation in:
(a) 1925 (b) 1927 (c) 1929 (d) 1933

337. Which of the following is not a function of money?
(a) Medium of exchange (b) Unit of account
(c) Standard of deferred payments
(d) Stabilisation of price level

338. Money has been defined as 'that by delivery of which debt contracts and price contracts are discharged, and in the shape of which general purchasing power is held'. Whose definition is this?
(a) G. Crowther (b) D.H. Robertson
(c) J.M. Keynes (d) George N. Halm

339. Fiat money refers to:
(a) Credit money (b) Legal money (c) Full-bodied money (d) International money

340. Which one of the following is an example of quasi-money or near-money?
(a) Bills of exchange (b) Cheques (c) Bank notes (d) Coins

341. When the commodity value of money and its value as money are equal, it is called:
(a) Token money (b) Full-bodied money
(c) Quasi-money (d) Fiat money

342. The limited legal-tender money stands for that component of money which:
(a) Is issued in a limited amount (b) Is legal tender for payment upto a certain maximum amount (c) Is legal tender in specified areas
(d) Is to be used in specific transactions

343. As compared to the classical theory, which function of money was stressed more in the Keynesian theory?
(a) Unit of account (b) Medium of exchange
(c) Standard of deferred payments (d) Store of value

344. 'Bad money drives good money out of circulation'. With whose name is this law associated?
(a) J.M. Keynes (b) Thomas Gresham
(c) L.E. Mises (d) R.G. Hawtrey

345. Identify the country which was the first to adopt the gold standard:
(a) UK (b) France (c) Germany (d) USA

346. During which decade of the nineteenth century did most European countries adopt the gold standard?
(a) Sixties (b) Seventies (c) Eighties
(d) Nineties

347. When did the UK finally abandon the gold standard?
(a) 1925 (b) 1929 (c) 1931 (d) 1936

348. Who is generally regarded as the founder of the Modern Quantity Theory of Money?

(a) J.M. Keynes (b) Milton Friedman (c) M.L. Bursten (d) Don Patinkin

349. The Quantity Theory of Money establishes the relationship between quantity of money in an economy and the level of:
(a) Employment (b) National income (c) Prices (d) Savings

350. Identify Pigou's cash balances equation:
(a) $M = Ky + K'A$ (b) $M = KPO$ (c) $M = KR/P$ (d) $M = PKT$

351. In the Fisher's equation of exchange $MV = PT$, what does T denote?
(a) Period of time (b) Volume of trade (c) Total money-wealth (d) Trend value of general price level

352. Cost-push inflation is caused by:
(a) Increase in the quantity of money (b) Increase in investment (c) Creation of credit money (d) Increase in the prices of inputs

353. Who introduced the concept of the real balance effect?
(a) A.C. Pigou (b) Alfred Marshall (c) J.M. Keynes (d) Milton Friedman

354. Which of the following according to Milton Friedman is not a key determinant of the demand for money?
(a) Aggregate wealth (b) Precautionary motive (c) Relative rates of return obtainable on different forms of assets (d) Physical non-human capital goods and human capital or wealth

355. The cash transactions approach to the quantity theory of money is usually associated with the name of:
(a) Alfred Marshall (b) Irving Fisher (c) J.M. Keynes (d) D.H. Robertson

356. The relationship between the market rate of interest and the market price of a bond is:
(a) Inverse (b) Direct (c) Positive and proportionate (d) Uncertain

357. The degree of elasticity in respect of speculative demand for money, under the liquidity trap conditions, is:
(a) Zero (b) One (c) Greater than one (d) Infinite

358. A retail price index is a good measure of changes in:
(a) Consumers' cost of living (b) General purchasing power of money (c) Average standard of living (d) Patterns of consumer expenditure

359. Which of the following is not an instrument of monetary policy?
(a) Taxation (b) Bank rate (c) Open-market operations (d) Credit rationing

360. At a very low rate of interest, the interest-elasticity of the speculative demand for money becomes:
(a) Low (b) High (c) Very high (d) Infinite

361. The liquidity trap condition occurs at a:
(a) Low rate of interest (b) Very low rate of interest (c) High rate of interest (d) Very high rate of interest

362. In which capacity does a person stand to gain from deflation?
(a) As a pensioner (b) As a debtor (c) As an entrepreneur (d) As an equity-holder

363. According to the classical approach, the demand for money primarily depends upon:
(a) Rate of interest (b) Economic transactions (c) Speculative activity (d) Precautionary motive

49

364. Which of the following measures is helpful in controlling inflation?
(a) Raising the bank rate (b) Price control and rationing of essential goods (c) Reduction of government expenditure (d) All of the above

365. During the period of hyper-inflation, there takes place astronomical rise in prices and, as a result, money becomes almost worthless. Such a situation was witnessed in Germany in 1923 and in China in:
(a) 1947 (b) 1949 (c) 1951 (d) 1953

366. Stagflation refers to a situation which is characterised by:
(a) Deflation and rising unemployment (b) Inflation and deflation (c) Sustained price-rise and rising unemployment (d) Stagnant employment and deflation

367. The first explanation of stagflation was offered originally in 1931 by:
(a) Friedrich A. von Hayek (b) J.M. Keynes (c) Bent Hansen (d) Milton Friedman

368. The reduction or elimination of inflation is known as:
(a) Disinflation (b) Deflation (c) Creeping inflation (d) Stagflation

369. Which of the following is not a function of a commercial bank?
(a) Accepting public deposits (b) Granting loans and advances (c) Undertaking agency functions (d) Banker to the Government

370. Which of the following is not a liability of commercial banks?
(a) Demand deposits (b) Time deposits (c) Advances from the central bank (b) Security holdings

371. Which is not a function of the central bank of a country?
(a) Lender of the last resort (b) Controller of credit (c) Custodian of nation's foreign exchange reserves (d) Supervisor of nation's fiscal policy

372. Under the unit banking system, each individual bank is a separate entity having its own independent management and board of directors. Which country is generally regarded as the home of the unit banking system?
(a) USA (b) Germany (c) France (d) Japan

373. The branch banking system is currently in vogue in most countries of the world. Identify the country where it first developed:
(a) South Africa (b) UK (c) Canada (d) Australia

374. The chain banking system a variant of the group banking system, developed around the mid-nineteenth century and reaching the apex of popularity in the present century. In which country did it develop?
(a) USA (b) UK (b) Germany (d) Italy

375. In which country was the instrument of minimum legal cash reserves ratio for banks first introduced?
(a) USA (b) UK (c) Germany (d) Japan

376. Which of the following is not a part of the unorganised Indian money market?
(a) Indigenous bankers (b) Co-operative credit societies (c) Chit funds (d) Money lenders

377. Which one of the following will reduce the capacity of commercial banks to lend?
(a) Sale of securities in the open market by the central bank (b) Reduction in the discount rate

(c) Reduction of the required cash reserves ratio (d) Purchase of securities by the Central bank in the open market

378. If there is a significant decrease in the demand for loans, banks will be forced to:
(a) Sell securities to the public (b) Adjust their portfolios (c) Resort to creating credit (d) Increase liquidity

379. Open market operations refer to the buying and selling of:
(a) Commercial bills (b) Foreign exchange (c) Gold (d) Government securities

380. Bank rate refer to the interest rate at which:
(a) Commercial banks receive deposits from the public (b) Central bank gives loans to commercial banks (c) Government loans are floated (d) Commercial banks grant loans to their customers

381. The immediate effect of credit-creation by banks is:
(a) Rise in prices (b) Increase in money supply (c) Increase in real national income (d) Reduction of poverty

382. Selective credit control devices are used by the central bank of a country to:
(a) Regulate the volume of aggregate bank credit in the economy (b) Regulate credit-creation on the part of some selected banks (c) Control the flow of aggregate bank credit to different productive activities in the economy (d) Selectively allocate credit among banks

383. In a bimetallic standard:
(a) Two metals (usually gold and silver) are simultaneously monetised and their monetary

values are fixed as legal tender (b) Both gold and silver coins circulate as unlimited legal tender (c) Coinage as well as exports and imports of both the metals are free (d) All of the above

384. One of the following is an instrument of qualitative credit control. Identify it:
(a) Credit rationing (b) Bank rate (c) Open market operations (d) Minimum statutory cash reserves ratio

385. Which of the following is an instrument of quantitative credit control?
(a) Credit rationing (b) Prescribing margin requirements (c) Variable reserve ratio (d) Consumer credit regulation

386. Arrange the following assets of a bank in the ascending order of income (i.e. in the descending order of liquidity): I-Bills; II-Loans; III-Investments in Government and other approved securities
(a) I, II, III (b) I, III, II (c) II, I, III (d) III, II, I

387. Which of the following is not an item on the assets side of the balance sheet of a commercial bank?
(a) Investments (b) Money at call and short notice (c) Reserves (d) Advances

388. Commercial banks have always to face a conflict between:
(a) Shareholders and depositors (b) Central bank and themselves (c) Liquidity and profitability (d) Demand deposits and time deposits

389. The main function of legal cash reserve requirements is to:

(a) Ensure safety of deposits (b) Influence the demand deposit-creating power of commercial banks (b) Regulate the inter-sectoral flow of money supply (d) Keep a portion of deposits liquid

390. Since when has the Reserve Bank of India been successfully operating the instrument of selective credit control in this country?
(a) 1939 (b) 1951 (c) 1956 (d) 1961

391. Identify the country which first employed credit rationing as an instrument of credit control:
(a) Germany (b) UK (c) USA (d) France

392. The 'terms of trade' refer to:
(a) Comparative advantage of one country over another in the production of a particular commodity (b) Bilateral trade agreements (c) Rates of exchange between two currencies (d) Ratio of the index of export prices to the index of import prices.

393. By which year had the gold standard virtually disappeared from the world as an international monetary system?
(a) 1933 (b) 1936 (c) 1939 (d) 1945

394. The market for very short term loans is known as:
(a) Capital market (b) Money market (c) Stock market (d) Discount market

395. If the increase in exports exceeds the increase in imports, and other things remain the same, then the level of income will:
(a) Rise (b) Remain the same (c) Fall (d) Move in an uncertain manner

396. Which of the following was not favoured by the mercantilists?

(a) Accumulation of gold by the country (b) Free trade (c) Export promotion (d) Import restriction

397. Of the following concepts of term of trade, which one was introduced by F.W. Taussig?
(a) Income terms of trade (b) Commodity terms of trade (c) Real cost terms of trade (d) Double factoral terms of trade

398. Dynamic factors in the realm of international trade theory relate to changes in:
(a) Income (b) Factor endowments (c) Technical knowledge and methods of production (d) All of the above

399. The devaluation of currency by a country is designed to lead to:
(a) Expansion of the export trade (b) Contraction of import trade (c) Promotion of import-substitution (d) All of these

400. What would be the impact on the country's balance of payments position, when in the context of inflationary pressures recourse is taken to expenditure reducing policies?
(a) Highly unfavourable (b) Unfavourable (c) Favourable (d) Neutral

401. Which of the following items in the balance of payments is invisible?
(a) Government expenditure abroad (b) Foreign investment (c) Foreign travel (d) Goods exported

402. If the elasticity of foreign demand for the country's exports is unity, the supply curve of foreign exchange will be:
(a) Backward bending (b) Vertical (c) Positively sloping from left to right (d) Horizontal

403. A deficit disequilibrium in the balance of payments can be corrected through:
(a) Devaluation (b) Monetary squeeze
(c) Exchange controls and import quotas
(d) All of the above

404. The spot and forward markets in foreign exchange are linked to each other through:
(a) Interest arbitrage (b) Hedging (c) Speculation (d) All of the above

405. What does the modern theory of international trade predict regarding difference in factor prices between nations on account of trade? The difference:
(a) Increases (b) Diminishes (c) Remains the same (d) Either diminishes or increases

406. The multiple exchange rates were first employed by:
(a) Brazil (b) Ecuador (c) Germany (d) Peru

407. Which of the following statements is not correct?
(a) Devaluation can have only temporary effects and it may provoke other countries to retaliate (b) Many countries of Europe resorted to exchange clearing agreements during the 1930s (c) The balance of payments of a country is a balance sheet showing the country's foreign assets and liabilities at any given period of time (d) The concept of single factoral terms of trade was developed by Jacob Viner

408. Under the flexible exchange rate system, the exchange rate is determined by:
(a) The central bank of the country (b) The forces of demand and supply in the foreign

exchange market (c) The price of gold (d) The purchasing power of currencies

409. The elasticity of demand for foreign exchange for financing capital outflow is:
(a) Zero (b) Greater than zero (c) One (d) Less than infinity

410. The foreign exchange market performs the function of:
(a) Transfer of purchasing power (b) Provisions of credit for financing foreign trade (c) Furnishing facilities for hedging foreign exchange risks (d) All of the above

411. According to the Heckscher-Ohlin theory of international trade the most important cause of differences in relative commodity prices and trade between nations is the differences in:
(a) Consumer tastes and preferences (b) Factor endowments (c) Knowledge and technology (d) Demand conditions

412. On which of the following is the law of comparative costs based?
(a) Labour theory of value (b) Opportunity cost theory (c) Law of diminishing returns (d) Both (a) and (b)

413. Which among the following, is not an assumption of the classical theory of comparative cost advantage?
(a) Labour is the only factor of production (b) Production takes place under diminishing returns (c) There are no tariffs (d) Prices are determined by their real labour costs of production

414. Developing countries usually complain of:
(a) Detoriation in their terms of trade (b) Serious hurdles in the way of export

promotion (c) Uncertainty and inadequacy of foreign aid (d) All of the above

415. Adam Smith's views on world trade can be best understood if one considers them as a reaction to:
(a) The mercantilist approach to trade (b) Ricardo's views on trade (c) The labour theory of value (d) None of the above

416. What proportion of international trade is based on absolute differences in costs of production?
(a) All (b) Substantial (c) Very little (d) Nil

VI

BUSINESS AND FINANCE

417. Business can be defined as:
(a) Selling of goods (b) Buying of goods (c) A market place (d) Trade, commerce and industry

418. What can be the maximum number of partners in a partnership firm?
(a) 10 (b) 15 (c) 20 (d) 25

419. Which form of business organisation would be most suitable for a capital intensive business?
(a) Sole proprietorship (b) Partnership (c) Co-operative society (d) Joint-stock company

420. According to the systems approach, a system is the:
(a) Sum total of all its components (b) Orderly arrangement of its components in a co-ordinated manner (c) A combination of some of the components (d) A systemic view of the organisation

421. A business organisation has constant and invisible interaction with its:
(a) Employees (b) Suppliers and customers (c) External environment (d) Government

422. The asset limit above which a company or group would be covered under the MRTP in India for concentration of economic power is:
(a) Rs 50 lakh (b) Rs 1 crore (c) Rs 20 crore (d) Rs 100 crore

423. Which one of the following refers to 'factoring services'?
(a) Guaranteeing realisation from debtors (b) Financing working capital (c) Providing project consultancy (d) None of the above

424. A consumer complaint is registered by the MRTP Commission in India on a complaint made by at least:
(a) 5 consumers (b) 25 consumers (c) 50 consumers (d) 100 consumers

425. Vertical combination implies:
(a) Formation of pools and cartels (b) Integration of enterprises engaged in different stages of production of a particular product (c) A group of organisations having common sales set-up (d) Integration of enterprises engaged in manufacturing similar products

426. An indirect tax is one where:
(a) Tax is levied on wealth (b) Tax is levied always on products (c) Points of impact and incidence are the same (d) Points of impact and incidence are different

427. Which one of the following is an example of indirect tax?
(a) Corporation tax (b) Wealth tax (c) Income tax (d) Sales tax

428. The incidence of tax refers to:
(a) The effect produced by the tax (b) The rate of taxation (c) One who bears the ultimate money burden of the tax (d) One who is immediately responsible to pay the tax

429. Who is generally regarded as the father of modern management?
(a) F.W. Taylor (b) Henry Fayol (c) James D. Mooney (d) Alan C. Reiley

430. The term Managerial Revolution refers to the prediction that with the expansion in size of business units, world affairs will eventually be in the hands of a few powerful managers. Who made use of this term?
(a) J. Burnham (b) F.W. Taylor (c) Alfred Marshall (c) J.K. Galbraith

431. The principle of scientific management implies:
(a) Replacement of rules of thumb by scientific principles of management (b) Managing business in a scientific way (c) Use of science in business (d) Human approach to management

432. Objectives in the context of management may be defined as:
(a) Laying down targets to be achieved over a period of time (b) The end result which an organisation tries to attain (c) The purpose for the organisation's survival (d) Parameters for unified planning

433. The two key factors in 'management by objectives' are:
(a) Performance evaluation and objectives (b) Democratic goal-setting and verifiable objectives (c) Systems approach and long-range planning (d) Short-run goods and flexibility

434. An informal organisation is one where:
(a) There is no division of work (b) Jobs of individuals are not precisely defined (c) The structure is not prescribed by formal authority (d) There are no fixed hours of work

435. The first level of needs in Maslow's 'need hierarchy' is:
(a) Social needs (b) Security needs (c) Physiological needs (d) Esteem needs

436. Planning and control are related in such a way that:
(a) Planning precedes control (b) Control precedes planning (c) Both are concurrent (d) Both go hand-in-hand with each other in a cyclical manner

437. Communication is complete when the:
(a) Message is sent by the sender (b) Message is received by the receiver (c) Message is received and understood by the receiver (d) Message is further transmitted by the receiver

438. A private company must have at least:
(a) 2 members (b) 5 members (c) 7 members (d) 10 members

439. Unless the Articles of Association otherwise provide, the quorum for a general meeting of a public company is:
(a) One-third of the total members (b) Five members personally present (c) Seven members personally present (d) Twenty members personally present

440. A Special Resolution is one which is passed in a general meeting by:

(a) A simple majority of votes (b) Two-third majority of votes (c) Three-fourth majority of votes (d) Three-fifth majority of votes

441. A share warrant can be issued by:
(a) Private companies only (b) Public companies only (c) Both public and private companies (d) Government companies only

442. What is the minimum number of shareholders necessary for a public company?
(a) 5 (b) 7 (c) 11 (d) 20

443. The share capital of a company refers to:
(a) Equity share capital (b) Preference share capital (c) Equity and preference share capital (d) Equity and preference share capital and debentures

444. Within how many days of the declaration of dividend must dividend warrants be posted to shareholders?
(a) 21 days (b) 30 days (c) 42 days (d) 60 days

445. In which year was the Indian Contract Act passed?
(a) 1850 (b) 1872 (c) 1926 (d) 1939

446. Any agreement by a minor which is beneficial to him is a:
(a) Void agreement (b) Illegal agreement (c) Valid contract (d) Void contract

447. The liability of partners in a partnership firm is:
(a) Joint and several (b) Joint and alternative (c) Alternative (d) Joint

448. What is the maximum number of partners necessary in a partnership firm carrying on banking business?
(a) 5 (b) 10 (c) 15 (d) 20

449. The suit for specific performance in case of breach of contract may be filed only where the subject matter relates to:
(a) Movable goods (b) Immovable property (c) Perishable goods (d) Personal skill and qualifications

450. Which one of the following is a void agreement?
(a) Agreement in restraint of trade (b) Agreement whose object is illegal (c) Agreement in respect of sale of goodwill (d) Service agreements containing negative stipulations during the tenure of service

451. Crossing a cheque 'Not Negotiable' affords security against:
(a) Negotiation of cheques (b) Theft of cheques (c) Payment to wrong banker or account (d) None of the above

452. Non-registration of a partnership does not affect the:
(a) Suit by a partner against the firm or other co-partners (b) Suit by the firm against third parties (c) Suit by third parties against the firm (d) Claim of set-off or other proceedings on a contract by the firm

453. Organisation Theory is concerned with the:
(a) Development of an organisation as an economic unit (b) Study to explain the nature and composition of organisations as a social or human group (c) Rules governing an organisation (d) Human behaviour at work

454. With which of the following is Behavioural Science in management related?
(a) Organisational response to its environment (b) Scientific study of human behaviour

(c) Superior-subordinate behaviour within an organisation (d) None of the above

455. Job-enrichment means:
(a) More tasks of the same general nature
(b) More tasks providing greater challenge
(c) Change or variation of job after a time period (d) None of the above

456. An organisation structure refers to the:
(a) Nature of superior-subordinate relationship (b) Relationships and dependencies within an organisation (c) Extent of delegation of authority in the organisation (d) Flow of authority and responsibility

457. Finance is concerned with:
(a) Arrangement of funds (b) Identification of sources of funds (c) Recording utilisation of funds (d) All of the above

458. Current Ratio is the ratio of:
(a) Current assets to current liabilities (b) Current liabilities to current assets (c) Fixed assets to total liabilities (d) Current assets to total liabilities

459. Debt Equity Ratio refers to the ratio of:
(a) Debtors to equity share capital (b) Long term debt to shareholders' equity (c) Total debt to equity share capital (d) Long term debt to equity share capital

460. 'Trading on equity' means:
(a) Use of equity share capital for trade financing (b) Use of fixed-interest borrowed funds for getting a higher return on equity (c) Having no borrowed funds (d) Trading in equity share capital

461. Cost of goods sold refers to:

(a) Sales minus gross profits (b) Sales minus profits (c) Cost of materials, labour and overheads (d) None of the above

462. In the pay-back period method of capital budgeting, investment is divided by:
(a) Annual profits (b) Return on investment (c) Constant annual cash flow (d) Cumulative cash flow

463. The relationship between EBIT and EPS gives:
(a) Operating leverage (b) Financial leverage (c) Normal leverage (d) Composite leverage

464. Break-even-point is a situation where:
(a) Profits are negative (b) There is no profit no loss (c) Profits-Costs (d) Business is at the point of dissolution

465. Under-capitalisation refers to a situation where:
(a) The capital base is larger for the earnings made (b) The capital base does not justify the amount of earnings made and needs to be enhanced (c) The capital base justifies the earnings made (d) The earnings ratio of the company equals the industry's earnings ratio

466. A schedule of balances drawn from the ledger is called:
(a) A trial balance (b) A balance sheet (c) A profit and loss account (d) A statement of account

467. Goodwill of a firm represents:
(a) Fixed assets (b) Tangible assets (c) Intangible assets (d) Fictitious assets

468. A bank account is a:
(a) Personal account (b) Real account (c) Liability account (d) Nominal account

469. Prepaid expenses appearing in a trial balance will figure in the:

(a) Balance sheet (b) Profit and loss account
(c) Profit and loss account and balance sheet
(d) Prepaid expenses account

470. Sale of old furniture on credit will appear in the:

(a) Sales day book (b) Cash book (c) Journal
(d) Debtors ledger

471. The excess of current assets over current liabilities is called:

(a) Net worth (b) Working capital (c) Net tangible worth (d) Turnover

472. Depreciation is the process of:

(a) Allocation of costs (b) Valuation of assets
(c) Use of assets (d) None of the above

473. What is the objective of cost accounting?

(a) Cost determination (b) Cost analysis
(c) Cost control (d) All of the above

474. What is Conversion Cost?

(a) Cost of materials and labour (b) Cost of transforming direct materials into finished products (d) Cost of labour (d) Total cost of running business

475. In an integrated costing system, most of the data relevant to cost accounting comes from the:

(a) Cost accounting system (b) Financial accounting system (c) Stores accounting system
(d) Sales and distribution system

476. Which method of costing is used by sugar mills?

(a) Unit or output costing (b) Job costing
(c) Process costing (d) Batch costing

477. Premium on redemption of debentures is accounted for in the:
(a) Personal account (b) Real account
(c) Nominal account (d) Assets account

478. After debentures are redeemed, the balance in the sinking fund account is transferred to:
(a) Capital reserve (b) General reserve
(b) Profit and loss account (d) Secret reserve

479. To the extent redemption of preference shares takes place out of profits, an equal amount has to be transferred to:
(a) Development rebate reserve (b) Capital redemption reserve (c) General reserve
(d) Share premium account

480. When shares are forfeited, the share capital account is debited by:
(a) Calls-in-arrears (b) Called-up amount
(c) Paid-up amount (d) Face value of shares

481. The profit on re-issuing forfeited shares is transferred to:
(a) Capital reserve (b) Capital redemption reserve (c) General reserve (d) Revaluation reserve

482. The share application account is a:
(a) Real account (b) Personal account
(c) Nominal account (d) Asset account

483. The excess of purchase price over net assets is:
(a) Goodwill (b) Capital reserve (c) Preliminary expense (d) Revenue reserve

484. In the balance sheet of a company, the items goodwill, patents and trade marks are shown under the heading:
(a) Current assets (b) Loans and advances
(c) Fixed assets (d) Investments

485. A preliminary expense is a:
(a) Current asset (b) Fictitious asset (c) Current liability (d) Non-current liability

486. Divisible profits do not include:
(a) Reserve fund (b) Profit on revaluation of assets (c) Post-incorporation profits (d) None of the above

487. Advance payment of tax should be shown on the:
(a) Assets side of a balance sheet (b) Liabilities side of a balance sheet (c) Debit side of a profit and loss account (d) Credit side of a profit and loss account

488. Dividends are usually paid on the:
(a) Called-up capital (b) Paid-up capital (c) Subscribed capital (d) Nominal capital

489. Which of the following is not concerned with the valuation of goodwill?
(a) Earning capacity method (b) Super profits method (c) Average profits method (d) Net assets method

490. When two or more companies dissolve to form a new company, the process is known as:
(a) Amalgamation (b) Absorption (c) Reconstruction (d) Combination

491. Absorption is said to take place when:
(a) A company is formed to take over another company (b) Two or more companies are dissolved to form a few company (c) Two or more companies dissolve to be taken over by an existing company (d) Two companies decide for virtual integration of their operations

492. For calculating market value using P/E ratios, it is necessary to know:

(a) The rate of dividend (b) Average profits (c) Market price of the share (d) Earnings per share and market price of the share

493. The relationship between normal rate of return and P/E ratio is:
(a) Inverse (b) Direct (c) Irregular (d) None of the above

494. For a company to carry out capital reduction, permission is required from the:
(a) Controller of Capital Issues (b) Competent Court (c) Company Law Board (d) Board of Directors

495. Any balance in the capital reduction account after writing off lost capital is transferred to:
(a) Capital reserve (b) General reserve (c) Debenture redemption reserve (d) Capital redemption reserve

496. In a scheme of reorganisation, the amount of shares surrendered by shareholders is transferred to the:
(a) Shares surrendered account (b) Capital reduction account (c) Capital reorganisation account (d) Capital sacrificed account

497. Amounts sacrificed by shareholders are credited to the:
(a) Capital reserve account (b) General reserve account (c) Capital reduction account (d) Capital redemption reserve account

498. At the commencement of winding up, a contributory is a:
(a) Creditor (b) Debtor (c) Shareholder (d) Debentureholder

499. The shareholding of the government in a government company must be at least:
(a) 33% (b) 50% (c) 51% (d) 100%

VII

NATIONAL INCOME ACCOUNTING

500. Which of the following is an economic activity?
(a) Medical facilities rendered by a charitable dispensary (b) Teaching one's own child at home (c) A housewife doing household duties (d) Listening to music on the radio

501. Which of the following is closest to the concept of economic production?
(a) Sale of goods and services for profit (b) Manufacture of goods (c) Addition to the value of commodities (d) Addition to the stock of goods and services for future use

502. Which of the following is a characteristic feature of a modern economy?
(a) Predominance of agriculture (b) Self-sufficient village economy (c) Diversity in production of commodities (d) Static technology

503. Identify economic stock from among the following:
(a) Depreciation of machinery (b) Production of food grains during the *Kharif* season (c) Purchase of food grains by a household (d) Bank deposit of a household

504. Which of the following is an economic flow?
(a) National capital (b) Demand for machinery (c) Current account of a household in a bank (d) Population of a country

505. A closed economy is one which:
(a) Does not trade with other countries (b) Does not possess any means of international transport (c) Does not have a coastal line (d) Is not a member of the United Nations Organisation

506. The traditional economy is characterised by:
(a) Division of labour and specialisation
(b) Organisation of production for self-consumption (c) Capital-intensive process of production (d) Increasing state intervention

507. Who among the following is a non-resident of India?
(a) A person of Indian origin working at the World Bank, Washington, DC (b) A person of Indian origin employed in the UNO office at New Delhi (c) The Indian manager of the Punjab National Bank branch office in London (d) An Indian tourist in Europe

508. Purchase of a ceiling fan by a household is treated in national income accounting as a part of:
(a) Capital formation (b) Consumption over a long period of time (c) Consumption at the time of its purchase (d) Intermediate consumption

509. Corporate enterprises refer to:
(a) Business houses maintaining a separate profit and loss account (b) Business houses that obtain loans from a bank (c) Business houses that obtain loans from the public (d) Business houses that are independent of their owners

510. Which of the following is not a corporate enterprise?
(a) Food Corporation of India (b) Municipal Corporation of Delhi (c) Tata Iron and Steel Company (d) Life Insurance Corporation of India

511. Departmental enterprises are a part of the:

(a) General government (b) Corporate sector (c) Non-profit public institutions (d) Non-profit institutions serving households

512. Which of the following is a departmental enterprise of the Government of India?
(a) Reserve Bank of India (b) Indian Oil Corporation (c) Indian Railways (d) Food Corporation of India

513. In which of the following sectors does production for self-consumption generally take place?
(a) Government administrative enterprises (b) Private corporate sector (c) Non-departmental public enterprises (d) Households

514. Subsistence production refers to:
(a) Production for self-consumption only (b) Production of necessities of life (c) Exports equalling imports (d) Low levels of production

515. Collective wants include:
(a) Sum total of all goods and services wanted by individuals (b) Goods like refrigerators shared by members of a family (c) Newspapers (d) Defence of a country

516. Which of the following are durable use producer-goods?
(a) Fertilisers (b) Tractors (c) Diesel oil (d) Fodder for cattle

517. Demand for intermediate consumption arises in:
(a) Consumer households (b) Government enterprises only (c) Corporate enterprises only (d) All producing sectors of the economy

518. Expenditure on the purchase of new replacement parts of machinery installed by a firm is part of:

(a) Fixed capital formation (b) Consumption of capital (c) Intermediate consumption (d) Final consumption

519. Which of the following is an expenditure on intermediate consumption?
(a) Purchase of coal by a steel factory (b) Purchase of coal by a dealer in coal (c) Purchase of coal by a household (d) All of the above

520. Demand for final consumption arises in:
(a) Household sector only (b) Government sector only (c) Both (a) & (b) (d) All sectors

521. Which of the following activities of a farmer is an example of intermediate consumption?
(a) Purchase of tractor (b) Payment of interest to a co-operative bank (c) Electricity charges for operating a pump (d) Wages paid to workers at harvesting time

522. Imputed rental value of owner occupied dwellings is a part of:
(a) Intermediate consumption (b) Capital formation (c) Final consumption (d) Expenditure on consumer durably

523. Sale of old newspapers by a household is a part of:
(a) Net final consumption expenditure of the household (b) Value added by the household sector (c) Capital formation (d) Transfer payments

524. Which of the following constitutes a part of domestic fixed capital formation?
(a) Net purchase of second-hand assets by corporate enterprises (b) Net purchase of second-hand physical assets from abroad (c) Expenditure on new parts of physical assets (d) Accumulation of stocks of fertilisers

525. Purchases made by the US Embassy in India are part of:
(a) Net factor earnings from abroad (b) Transfer payments (c) Domestic consumption expenditure (d) Exports from India to the USA

526. Direct purchases abroad made by the government on current account are a part of:
(a) Final consumption (b) Investments (c) Net factor payments abroad (d) Current transfers from the rest of the world

527. Which of the following is not a part of net investment in an economy?
(a) Purchase of old shares (b) Purchase of a wall-clock by a factory (c) Purchase of wall-clock by a household (d) Increasing the storage of raw materials

528. Which of the following is included in the consumption of fixed capital?
(a) Fall in the price of machinery and other stocks (b) Expenditure on repairs and maintenance (c) Destruction of buildings in an earthquake (d) Normal wear and tear of machinery while in use

529. Gross domestic fixed-capital formation does not include:
(a) Net purchase of second hand machinery by private corporate sector from Government (b) Net imports of second-hand machinery from abroad (c) Own account production of new assets (d) Construction of new roads and bridges

530. Value of output differs from the value added by the amount of:

(a) Indirect taxes (b) Wages and Salaries (c) Intermediate consumption (d) Gifts received from abroad

531. The gross fixed investment in an economy during a year is Rs 200 crore. The economy possessed Rs 1200 crore worth of fixed capital at the beginning of the year and the rate of depreciation is 10% per annum. What is the net value of fixed capital stock held at the end of the year?
(a) Rs 1600 crore (b) Rs 920 crore (c) Rs 1280 crore (d) Rs 1200 crore

532. If consumption of capital is equal to gross fixed investment, then:
(a) Net investment is zero (b) Net investment is negative (c) Net investment is positive (d) National income is constant

533. Which of the following constitutes an investment by a household?
(a) Purchasing a washing machine (b) Painting a house (c) Purchasing a new house (d) Purchasing a new car

534. Net value added is equal to:
(a) Payments accruing to factors of production (b) Compensation of employees (c) Wages plus rent plus interest (d) Value of output minus depreciation

535. Addition to the stocks of foodgrains by the Food Corporation of India is a part of:
(a) Net fixed investment (b) Net revenue of the Government sector (c) Gross capital formation (d) Final consumption

536. Mixed income of the self-employed means:
(a) Gross profits received by a proprietorship (b) Rent interest and profit of an enterprise

(c) Combined factor payments which are not distinguishable (d) Wages due to family workers

537. Operating surplus implies:
(a) Gross value added minus profits (b) Net income from property and entrepreneurship (c) Net profits of public enterprises (d) Part of profits which are reinvested

538. Operating surplus arises in:
(a) Government sector only (b) Household sector only (c) Public enterprises only (d) All producing enterprises in the corporate sector

539. Operating surplus differs from net value added by the amount of:
(a) Compensation of employees (b) Net indirect taxes (c) Consumption of fixed capital (d) Dividends

540. Which of the following is not a part of the compensation of employees?
(a) Employer's contribution to provident fund (b) Leave travel allowance (c) Payments made to visiting foreign consultant (d) Pensions to retired employees

541. Identify the item which is not a factor payment:
(a) Free uniforms to defence personnel (b) Salaries and allowance to the members of Parliament (c) Imputed rent of an owner-occupied building (d) Scholarships given to scheduled caste students

542. Which of the following is an example of factor-income from abroad?
(a) Interest earned by a non-resident Indian on his bank account in India (b) Export of handicrafts from India to the UK (c) Money

sent by an engineer employed in London to his family in Delhi (d) Profits earned by a branch of the State Bank of India in London

543. Transfer payments refer to payments which are made:
(a) Without any exchange of goods and services (b) To workers on transfer from one job to another (c) As compensation of employees (d) Non of the above

544. Personal disposable income is.
(a) Always equal to personal income (b) Always more than personal income (c) Equal to personal income minus direct taxes paid by household (d) Equal to personal income minus indirect taxes

545. If during a year the national income at constant prices goes up by 5%, while prices also rise by 5% and population registers a growth of 2%; then the real per capita income will:
(a) Remain constant (b) Rise by 2% (c) Decrease by 3% (d) Increase by 3%

546. National income estimates of India are published both at current and constant prices. What is the base year for constant price estimates published at present?
(a) 1960-61 (b) 1970-71 (c) 1980-81 (d) 1985-86

547. In national income accounts, direct personal taxes are recorded as:
(a) Receipts of the government sector and payments of the corporate sector (b) Receipts of the government sector and payments of the household sector (c) Transfer from the household sector to the government sector (d) Disbursements of the government sector

548. For which of the following sectors is the income method used for estimation of national income of India?
(a) Agriculture and allied activities (b) Fishing (c) Forestry (d) Banking and insurance

549. Identify the sector in respect of which the expenditure method is used for estimating national income in India:
(a) Registered manufacturing (b) Construction (c) Public administration and defence (d) Real estate, ownership of dwellings and business services

550. If GNP at market prices is Rs 1200 crore, and fixed capital stock is worth Rs 2000 crore which depreciates at the rate of 10% per annum and the net indirect taxes amount is Rs 150 crore. What is the national income?
(a) Rs 3050 crore (b) Rs 2850 crore (c) Rs 1000 crore (d) Rs 850 crore

551. National income differs from the net national product at market prices by the amount of:
(a) Current transfers from rest of the world (b) Net indirect taxes (c) National debt interest (d) It does not differ

552. If net factor income from abroad is zero, then:
(a) Domestic product is zero (b) National product is zero (c) National product is equal to domestic product (d) National product is constant

553. For the estimation of private income which of the following items has to be added to national income?
(a) Income from property accruing to government (b) Savings of the non-departmental

enterprises (c) Subsidies (d) Interest on national debt

554. While estimating personal income from national income, which of the following items need to be deducted?
(a) Net indirect taxes (b) Direct taxes paid by households (c) Dividends (d) Corporate profits tax

555. Which of the following has to be added to national income to obtain the net national disposable income?
(a) Income from property and entrepreneurship accruing to Government (b) Net current transfers from the rest of the world (c) Profits of public enterprises (d) Loans from public

556. Net national product at factor cost is:
(a) Equal to national income (b) More than national income (c) Less than national income (d) Always more than the gross national product

557. Which of the following is deducted while estimating national income by the value-added method?
(a) Value of goods and services produced for self-consumption (b) Imputed rental value of owner-occupied building (c) Net factor income from abroad (d) Consumption of capital

558. While estimating national income by the income method one of the following is not included. Identify it:
(a) Mixed income of the self employed (b) Inheritance tax or death duty (c) Interest on bonds of a foreign company (d) Income of employees of voluntary organisations

559. Which of the following is not included while estimating national income by the expenditure methods?
(a) Investment in shares of a new company
(b) Defence expenditure (c) Net indirect taxes
(d) Net exports

560. The difference between net national product at market prices and net domestic product at market prices is equal to:
(a) Value of exports (b) Net current transfers from abroad (c) Value of exports minus value of imports (d) Net factor income from abroad

561. Which of the following accounts for the difference between net domestic product at market prices and national income?
(a) Net factor income from abroad (b) National debt interest (c) Net factor income from abroad minus current transfers (d) Net factor income from abroad minus indirect taxes

562. Which of the following has to be deducted from the value of output to arrive at the net value added by a producing enterprise?
(a) Value of intermediate consumption
(b) Consumption of fixed capital (c) Net indirect taxes (d) All of the above

563. The value added method of measuring national income is also known as:
(a) Net output method (b) Production method (c) Industry of origin method (d) All of the above

564. Net borrowings from abroad are a part of:
(a) Gross domestic product (b) Net national product (c) Gross investment (d) Capital transfers

565. Aggregate gross receipts means:

(a) Turnover value of output (b) Receipts of the Government (c) Receipts of the corporate sector (d) Receipts from the rest of the world

566. The term national income commonly refers to:
(a) GNP at factor cost (b) GNP at market prices (c) NNP at factor cost (d) NNP at market prices

567. Which of the following is an example of transfer payment by the Government?
(a) Free housing accommodation to the government employees (b) Free housing accommodation to the President of India (c) National debt interest (d) Bonus paid to railway employees

568. Transfer receipts of the Government include:
(a) Sale of second hand cars by government departments (b) Direct and indirect taxes (c) Imputed rent of government buildings (d) Dividends received from public enterprises

569. Which one is an example of capital transfer within a country?
(a) Compensation to residents whose houses have been damaged by floods (b) Old age pensions (c) Interest paid by consumer households on consumer loans (d) Gifts to sick and poor on festivals

570. Net retained earnings abroad means:
(a) Income retained by a resident working abroad (b) Profits of resident companies abroad (c) Net undistributed profits of resident and non-resident companies (d) Foreign exchange reserves

571. Which of the following is not an example of capital transfers between countries?

(a) War damages (b) Gifts for cyclone victims (c) Economic aid (d) Grants from other governments

572. Interest on public debt is a part of:
(a) Transfer payments by the government (b) Transfer payments by enterprises (c) Domestic income (d) Interest payments by households

573. Which of the following is not a government transfer payment to households?
(a) Scholarship (b) Subsidy (c) Family pension (d) Unemployment allowance

574. Income from property is a part of:
(a) Mixed income of the self-employed (b) Operating surplus (c) Compensation of employees (d) None of these

575. Unilateral payments are known as:
(a) Factor income (b) Factor payments (c) Transfer payments (d) Payments for productive services rendered by others

576. Identify the correct statement:
(a) Personal disposable income excludes direct taxes paid by households (b) Capital transfers are paid from current income (c) Lottery income received by a household is factor income (d) Royalties are a part of compensation to employees

577. Which of the following includes interest on national debt?
(a) National income (b) Personal income (c) Gross national product (d) Net national product

578. Which of the following is incorrect?
(a) GDP at market prices = GDP at factor cost plus net indirect taxes (b) NNP at factor cost

= NNP at market prices minus net indirect taxes (c) GNP at market prices = GDP at market prices plus net factor income from abroad (d) None of the above

579. The first estimate of national income in India was made by Dadabhai Naoroji for the year:
(a) 1857-58 (b) 1867-68 (c) 1881-82 (d) 1890-91

580. Domestic incomes refer to incomes which are generated:
(a) By all the producers within the geographical territory of the country (b) By resident producers only (c) In the household sector (d) In cottage industries

581. If the general price level goes up by 12% and national income at constant prices increases by 3%, then the national income at current prices:
(a) Increase by 9% (b) Increase by 15% (c) Increase by 12% (d) Increase by 9%

582. Gross domestic product differs from net domestic product by the amount of:
(a) Government income from property (b) Net indirect taxes (c) Consumption of fixed capital (d) Net capital formation

VIII
ECONOMIC GROWTH AND DEVELOPMENT

583. Which of the following is generally regarded as the true index of economic growth?
(a) An increase in national income at constant prices during a year (b) A sustained increase in real per capita income (c) An increase in national income at current prices over time

(d) An increase in national income along with a corresponding increase in population

584. The concept of economic growth is:
(a) Identical with the concept of economic development (b) Narrower than the concept of economic development (c) Wider as compared to that of economic development (c) Unrelated to the concept of economic development

585. Which of the following is not an indicator of economically underdeveloped countries?
(a) Low per capita income (b) High death-rate (c) Low proportion of labour force in the primary sector (b) High level of illiteracy

586. The rate of growth of an economy mainly depends upon:
(a) The rate of growth of the labour force (b) The proportion of national income saved and invested (c) The rate of technological improvements (d) All of the above

587. Among the following determinants of growth, which is a non-economic factor?
(a) Natural resources (b) Population growth (c) Favourable legislation (d) Capital accumulation

588. Besides increase in output, economic development is concerned with:
(a) Inputs and their efficiency (b) Equitable distribution of income (c) Life sustenance, self-esteem and freedom from want, ignorance and squalor (d) All of the above

589. The stationary state as envisaged by Adam Smith, is marked by:
(a) Low rate of profit (b) Subsistence level wages (c) High rents (d) All of the above

590. Which of the following is inconsistent with Adam Smith's theory of development?
(a) Development process is cumulative in nature (b) There is no limit to the growth process (c) Capital accumulation and market extension are two prerequisites for output expansion (d) There should be no government interference in the working of the economy

591. The division of labour, according to Adam Smith, is limited by:
(a) The extent of the market (b) The quantity of capital available (c) Both (a) and (b) (d) The size of labour force

592. Among the various determinants of the growth of national wealth Adam Smith accorded central place to:
(a) Division of labour (b) Capital (c) Natural resources (d) Technology

593. Who put forward the theory of social dualism?
(a) A. Lewis (b) G. Myrdal (c) J.H. Boeke (d) A.O. Hirshman

594. Who coined the phrase 'demonstration effect'?
(a) W.W. Rostow (b) James Duessenberry (c) R. Nurkse (d) J.K. Galbraith

595. To achieve full economic growth, Malthus laid special emphasis on the proper combination of:
(a) Production and distribution (b) Natural resources and capital (c) Labour and technology (d) Production and trade

596. What according to Malthus puts a stop to the growth process?
(a) Inadequacy of capital accumulation (b) Deficiency in effective demand (c) Rapid

population growth (d) Operation of diminishing returns in agriculture

597. Identify the main factor which according to Malthus makes an economy move downwards in the long run to the subsistence level:
(a) Population pressure (b) Overproduction (c) Excess savings (d) Exploitation of workers

598. Which of the following measures, according to Malthus, would be helpful in raising and maintaining demand at a higher level?
(a) Maintaining unproductive consumption of luxury goods (b) Expansion of internal and external trade (c) Ensuring employment to the poor in public works (d) All of the above

599. Which of the following statements is not correct in the light of the Malthusian theory of growth?
(a) Growth of income cannot take place on its own (b) Population tends to increase in response to rise in income (c) There can be no general glut or overproduction in the market (d) Excess savings on the part of capitalists is the cause of overproduction

600. Which of the following statements is not in agreement with the Malthusian view on economic growth?
(a) The process of economic growth is automatic (b) Deficiency in effective demand halts the growth process (c) Lasting equilibrium can only be at the subsistence level (d) Savings are desirable only upto the limit set by the existence of profitable opportunities for investment

601. Which sector was emphasised most by Ricardo in the context of economic growth?

(a) Trade (b) Industry (c) Agriculture
(d) Services

602. In the Ricardian scheme of things, savings are provided by:
(a) Labourers (b) Capitalists (c) Landlords
(d) Both (b) and (c)

603. Which one of the following, according to Ricardo, would form a bottleneck to economic growth?
(a) Shortage of land (b) Rising rent
(c) Shortage of gold and silver (d) Rising wage bills

604. Which one of the following statements is not in tune with the Ricardian theory of growth?
(a) Rent tends to rise (b) Money wages tend to rise (c) Profits tend to fall (d) Profits tend to rise

605. Which one of the following is not an assumption of the Ricardian theory?
(a) Rising real wages (b) Fixity of land
(c) Operation of the law of diminishing returns
(d) Perfect competition

606. Which of the following policy-prescriptions for economic growth was suggested by Ricardo?
(a) Government's active participation in the economic field (b) Free trade in commodities
(c) Control over population growth
(d) Regulation of competition

607. In the Ricardian system, a crucial role in development was assigned to:
(a) Specialisation (b) Technological changes
(c) Profits (d) Government

608. The stationary state according to Malthus and Ricardo, is characterised by:

(a) The disappearance of profits (b) Net investment falling to zero (c) Wages coinciding with the subsistence level (d) All of the above

609. Which of the following is not a part of the classical theory of economic development?
(a) Labour supply would increase with rise in wages (b) Stationary state (c) Government interference (d) Capital accumulation is the basic cause of growth

610. Which of the following had the approval of the classical economists (particularly J.S. Mill) as an aid to development?
(a) Subsidising the poor (b) Imposition of temporary duties on imports to develop particular industries (c) Regulation of activities of the rising business class (d) Appropriating a part of the national product by the government for unproductive uses

611. The classical theory of economic development is of relevance for the less developed countries today because it lays emphasis on:
(a) Need for favourable institutional and social initiatives (b) Extension of markets (c) Capital accumulation (d) All of the above

612. According to the neo-classical theory, economic development is:
(a) Gradual (b) Harmonious (c) Cumulative (d) All of the above

613. Unemployment created by some long-term change in demand or technological conditions in an economy is known as:
(a) Frictional unemployment (b) Cyclical unemployment (c) Structural unemployment (d) Disguised unemployment

614. Arrange the following Rostow's stages of economic growth in their proper sequence:
I. Traditional society; II. Take-off stage; III. Age of mass consumption; IV. Drive to maturity
(a) I, II, IV, III (b) I, II, III, IV (c) II, I, IV, III (d) II, I, III, IV

615. How many stages of economic growth were defined and analysed by Rostow which all economies are supposed to pass through in the course of their development?
(a) Seven (b) Five (c) Four (d) Three

616. What causes development in terms of Rostow's theory?
(a) Favourable propensities of people (b) Changing profile of leading sectors of the economy (c) A sharp rise in investment (d) All of the above

617. Identify the country which was the first to move to the stage of high mass consumption:
(a) UK (b) USA (c) Germany (d) France

618. The take-off stage is characterised by:
(a) Rise in the rate of productive investment from 5% to over 10% of national income (b) Development of one or more substantial manufacturing sectors with a high growth rate (c) Quick emergence of a political, social and institutional framework to enable expansion in various fields (a) All of the above

619. Under the 'big-push' strategy of development, large investments are to be directed towards:
(a) Agriculture (b) Industry (c) Power (d) Transport

620. The basic logic behind the 'big-push' strategy of development is related to:

(a) Internal economies (b) External economies (c) An optimum combination (d) Both (a) and (b)

621. In the context of which region was the 'big-push' strategy of development formulated?
(a) South Asia (b) South-East Asia (c) Eastern Europe (d) East Africa

622. The 'big-push' strategy of development was first advocated by:
(a) Paul N. Rosenstein-Rodan (b) Simon Kuznets (c) W.A. Lewis (d) A.O. Hirshman

623. The justification of the 'big-push' strategy which involves concentrated efforts in the form of investments on a large scale is based on:
(a) Indivisibilities of demand (b) Complimentarity of demand (c) Skill formulation (d) All of the above

624. The capital-output ratio in developed countries is:
(a) Generally fluctuating (b) Fairly stable (c) Rigidly stationary (d) Gradually increasing

625. The incremental capital-output ratio (ICOR) refers to the:
(a) Ratio of investment to change in output (b) Ratio of capital stock to the total output (c) Marginal productivity of capital (d) Relationship between investment that is financed by the citizens of a country and the income enjoyed by them

626. The capital-output ratio is determined by:
(a) Sectoral allocation of capital (b) Level of economic activity (c) Human and natural resources (d) All of the above

627. Which growth model inspired the use of capital-output ratio for development planning?

(a) The Harrod-Domar model (b) Solow's model (c) Kaldor's model (d) Feldman's model

628. The capital-output ratio in a country during the different phases of growth:
(a) Remains unchanged (b) Fluctuates widely (c) Changes within narrow limits (d) Shows a secular declining trend

629. As an aid to development planning, much use is being made today of the input-output analysis. Who first used it?
(a) H. Liebenstein (b) W.W. Leontief (c) W.A. Lewis (d) A.O. Hirschman

630. Match the following:
I. Input-output analysis (A) W.W. Leontief
II. Stages of economic growth (B) R. Nurkse
III. Vicious circle of poverty (C) H. Liebenstein IV. Critical minimum effort (D) W.W. Rostow
(a) I-A, II-D, III-B, IV-C (b) I-C, II-B, III-D, IV-A (c) I-B, II-C, III-A, IV-D (d) I-D, II-A, III-C, IV-B

631. Which of the following statements is incorrect?
(a) The essence of balanced growth is that the economy should advance at a steady rate with savings equal to investment (b) The thesis of development with unlimited supplies of labour was originally formulated by R. Nurkse (c) The capital-output ratio is the inverse of the annual rate of return on productivity of capital (d) E.D. Domar assumed that full employment of labour and capital occurred simultaneously

632. Balanced growth implies:
(a) Simultaneous development of a variety of activities which support one another (b) Equal allocation of resources to different sectors

91

(c) Different sectors growing at their natural rates of growth (d) Uniform rate of growth of output over time

633. Development with unlimited supplies of labour hypothesis was originally formulated by:
(a) Gustav Ranis (b) W.A. Lewis (c) R. Nurkse (d) J. Schumpeter

634. Which of the following is not correctly matched?
(a) Big-push strategy: Paul N. Rosenstein-Rodan (b) Balanced growth theory: R. Nurkse (c) Development with unlimited supplies of labour: A.O. Hirschman (d) Critical minimum strategy: H. Liebenstein

635. If the capital-output ratio is 4 : 1 and the annual growth rate of population is 2.5%, what will be required rate of investment in the economy in order to achieve 3% growth per annum in per capita income?
(a) 30% (b) 20% (c) 15% (d) 12%

636. With economic growth, the proportion of labour-force engaged in agriculture:
(a) Increases (b) Decreases (c) Remains unaffected (d) Changes in an uncertain manner

637. A strategy of heavy industry is sometimes preferred for a developing economy because it can:
(a) Generate employment opportunities on a large scale (b) Provide a strong base for rapid industrialisation (c) Contain inflationary pressures (d) Meet deficits in balance of payments in the short-run

638. In which sphere are shadow prices particularly useful?

(a) Project evaluation and cost-benefit analyses (b) Calculation of surplus value (c) Sales policy of firms (d) Consumers equilibrium

639. Identify the economist who first advocated a rolling plan for developing countries?
(a) J. Robinson (b) N. Kaldor (c) G. Myrdal (d) Paul A. Samuelson

640. Which of the following is inconsistent with the Schumpeter's theory of development?
(a) The course of growth is continuous (b) The output expansion, initiated by the entrepreneur, increases in size with time, making it cumulative (c) Growth takes place on account of entrepreneurs who, with the help of bank credit, invest in innovative activity (d) Capitalism destroys itself by being successful through the erosion of its institutions, by the hostility of its intellectuals and other elite classes, and also by the weakening of entrepreneurial innovation

641. According to the Schumpeter's model, the innovating entrepreneurs get the necessary finance from:
(a) Voluntary savings (b) Own resources (c) Bank credit (d) Government

642. Which one of the following was given a central place by Schumpeter in his theory of development?
(a) Capital accumulation (b) Role of the Government (c) Need for balanced growth (d) Role of innovations

643. With which of the following kinds of dualism is H. Myint particularly associated with?

(a) Technological dualism (b) Geographical dualism (c) Financial dualism (d) Social dualism

644. Who formulated the theory of circular and cumulative causation which explains the perpetuation of underdevelopment through growing inequalities between developed and the underdeveloped countries?
(a) A. Lewis (b) Gunnar Myrdal (c) B. Higgins (d) J.H. Boeke

645. The second stage of the theory of demographic transition is characterised by:
(a) High birth-rate and high death-rate
(b) High birth-rate and falling death-rate
(c) Low birth-rate and low death-rate (d) Falling birth-rate and falling death-rate

646. Which of the following concepts, which are now extensively used in growth economics, was first formulated by Keynes?
(a) Marginal propensity to consume (b) Marginal propensity to save (c) Marginal efficiency of capital (d) All of the above

647. According to Keynesian economics, saving and investment are brought into equilibrium by variations in:
(a) Income (b) Price (c) Consumption (d) Output

648. Two economists have been particularly associated with the formulation of development with surplus labour hypothesis. One is R. Nurkse. Who is the other?
(a) W.A. Lewis (b) James S. Duessenberry (c) W.W. Rostow (d) Simon Kuznets

649. Perspective planning refers to:

(a) Indicative planning (b) Annual planning (c) Structural planning (d) Long-term planning

650. J.E. Meade pointed out three principal means of growth. Which of the following is not on the list?
(a) Growth of working population (b) Capital accumulation (c) Devaluation (d) Technical progress

651. The Harrod-Domar model is one of the well known models of growth. Which of the two authors of this model wrote earlier and in which year?
(a) Domar in 1940 (b) Harrod in 1939 (c) Domar in 1946 (d) Domar in 1948

652. Which of the following models formed the basis of India's Second Five Year Plan?
(a) Harrod-Domar model (b) Raj-Sen model (c) Cambridge model (d) Mahalanobis model

653. Which of the following models makes the assumption of constant saving-income ratio?
(a) Kaldor model (b) Leontief model (c) Harrod-Domar model (d) Joan Robinson model

654. Identify the model which is concerned with the 'golden age' equilibrium:
(a) Kaldor model (b) Joan Robinson model (c) Keynesian model (d) Domar model

655. Some models focus their attention on the maximum rate of growth at which the economy can grow. Which of the following models is of this type?
(a) Keynesian model (b) Hicks model (c) von-Neumann model (d) Solow model

656. Identify the model which analyses the contribution of technological progress to the overall growth rate:
(a) Solow model (b) Kaldor model (c) Harrod model (d) Tobin model

657. Which of the following is a two-sector model?
(a) Solow model (b) Harrod-Domar model (c) Joan Robinson model (d) Keynesian model

658. There is a model of inter-industrial relations where technological relations between industries are assumed to remain constant. Which one is it?
(a) Mahalanobis model (b) Feldman model (c) Leontief model (d) Lewis model

659. India's First Five Year Plan was based on:
(a) Mahalanobis model (b) Feldman model (c) Harrod-Domar model (d) Leontief model

660. Which of the following models uses three distinct concepts of stages of growth?
(a) Ramsey model (b) Harrod model (c) Domar model (d) Lewis model

661. Marx refers to the concept of organic composition of capital. Which of the following ratios stands for this capital?
Constant capital = C; Variable capital = V; Surplus value = S
(a) C/(V+S) (b) C/V (c) C/(C+V) (d) (C+V)/V

662. Marx had given a concept of unemployment in the context of the capitalist system which keeps wages down or prevents wages from rising even as demand for labour increases. What is that concept called?
(a) Surplus labour (b) Reserve army of labour (c) Under employment (d) Disguised unemployment

663. Marx attributed the capitalist crisis to:
(a) High rate of wages (b) Falling rate of profit
(c) Inflationary pressures (d) Exploitation of
labour

664. According to R. Nurkse, the inducement to invest in the context of an underdeveloped
economy is limited mainly by the:
(a) Lack of savings (b) Size of the market
(c) Lack of investment opportunities (d) Low
productivity of labour

IX

ECONOMIC AND COMMERCIAL
GEOGRAPHY

665. Which is the smallest continent?
(a) Europe (b) Antarctica (c) South America
(d) Australia

666. Asia is the largest continent in the world.
Roughly what percentage of the earth's area is
covered by it?
(a) 33.4 (b) 29.5 (c) 27.6 (d) 25.8

667. Which country in Europe has the largest area?
(a) Spain (b) France (c) Sweden (d) Finland

668. Identify the world's largest island:
(a) Greenland (b) New Guinea (c) Borneo
(d) Great Britain

669. Which is the highest waterfall in the world?
(a) Tugela (b) Utigord (c) Angel (d) Yosemite

670. Which is the world's largest river?
(a) Nile (b) Amazon (c) Hudson (d) Mississippi-
Missouri

671. Which is the biggest ocean in the world?

(a) Arctic Ocean (b) Indian Ocean (d) Pacific Ocean (d) Atlantic Ocean

672. Which two continents are complementary to each other?
(a) Africa and South America (b) Asia and Australia (c) North America and South America (d) Asia and Europe

673. Which of the following is a block mountain?
(a) Andes (b) Rockies (c) Alps (d) Vosges

674. Which is the world's smallest independent country?
(a) Monaco (b) Vatican city (d) Naura (d) Turalu

675. Which place is known as the Land of Thousand Lakes?
(a) Norway (b) Sweden (c) Finland (d) Srinagar

676. Which country is the leading producer of wood pulp in the world?
(a) Canada (b) USSR (c) USA (d) Japan

677. Which of the following resources is inexhaustible?
(a) Natural gas (b) Iron ore (c) Coal (d) Solar energy

678. Identify the country which is the largest among coal producing countries in the world:
(a) USA (b) China (c) UK (d) France

679. Brazil leads in the production of:
(a) Tea (b) Coffee (c) Cotton (d) Tobacco

680. Identify the country which is known as the sugar bowl of the world:
(a) Cuba (b) Colombia (c) India (d) Peru

681. Which country has the highest dam?
(a) Canada (b) Egypt (c) China (d) USSR

682. Two countries produce about 40% of the world's wine. France is one of them. Which is the other?

(a) Spain (b) USSR (c) Italy (d) Turkey

683. Which is the largest producer and exporter of palm oil in the world?

(a) Indonesia (b) Mexico (c) Zaire (d) Malaysia

684. What is New Zealand's extent of dependence on water power as a source of electricity?

(a) 45% (b) 55% (c) 65% (d) 75%

685. Two countries lead the world in bauxite production. Guinea is one. Which is the other?

(a) Brazil (b) Australia (c) Jamaica (d) USSR

686. Which country is the leading producer of silver in the world?

(a) USSR (b) USA (c) South Africa (d) China

687. Which of the following minerals does not contain any metal?

(a) Silver ore (b) Lead ore (c) Aluminium ore (d) Mica ore

688. Identify the country which is the leading iron ore producer in the world?

(a) USA (b) USSR (c) France (d) Australia

689. Which of the following prevents deserts from spreading further?

(a) Afforestation (b) Constructing canals (c) Deforestation (d) Desalination

690. Where are Savanna grasslands found?

(a) Africa (b) North America (b) Canada (d) Australia

691. Identify the country which leads in world fish production:

(a) China (b) USA (c) USSR (d) Japan

692. Which country is the largest producer of nuclear power in the world?
(a) USA (b) France (c) USSR (d) Japan

693. Which country has the largest share in cotton production?
(a) USA (b) China (c) USSR (d) Pakistan

694. Which one of the following cities is known as the 'city of skyscrapers'?
(a) New York (b) Ottawa (c) Tokyo (d) Washington

695. Which of the following fertilisers is used after sowing seeds?
(a) Potash (b) Phosphorus (c) Nitrate (d) Green manure

696. Which is the world's largest producer and consumer of synthetic rubber?
(a) Malaysia (b) USA (c) Indonesia (d) Thailand

697. Which is the leading country in pipeline transportation of crude petroleum?
(a) USSR (b) Iraq (c) Iran (d) USA

698. The Richter Scale is used for measuring:
(a) Earthquake's magnitude (b) Intensity of wind (c) Depth of ocean (d) Height of mountain

699. Identify the first metal used by man:
(a) Gold (b) Iron (c) Copper (d) Aluminium

700. The Duncan Passage is between:
(a) Sri Lanka and India (b) Andaman Islands and Nicobar Islands (c) Pakistan and Afghanistan (d) China and India

701. Which is the world's largest city?
(a) Tokyo (b) Seoul (c) Shanghai (d) Moscow

702. What was the earlier name of Zimbabwe?

(a) Zanzibar (b) Rhodesia (c) South West Africa (d) Bechuanaland

703. Which country is known as the Playground of Europe?
(a) France (b) Switzerland (c) Holland (d) Sweden

704. Mesopotamia was the old name of:
(a) Iran (b) Iraq (c) Saudi Arabia (d) United Arab Republic

705. The cultivation of which crop requires water-logging?
(a) Rice (b) Cotton (c) Pulses (d) Oilseeds

706. Mixed farming refers to:
(a) Growing a series of crops on the same piece of land (b) Agriculture under which crop production is combined with livestock raising (c) Farming in which food and commercial crops are mixed (d) Farming wherein vegetables and crop are grown

707. With an average of 50 cm of rain in a tropical place, which of the following crops would be most suitable for a farmer to grow?
(a) Rice (b) Wheat (c) Sugarcane (d) Jowar

708. Which is the largest rice producing country in the world?
(a) China (b) USSR (c) India (d) Indonesia

709. China is the largest tobacco producing country in the world. Its percentage share in the world is:
(a) 35 (b) 30 (c) 25 (d) 20

710. What is approximately the total perimeter of India?
(a) 14,500 km (b) 14,900 km (c) 15,200 km (d) 15,600 km

711. About how many times is the area of India smaller than that of China?
    (a) Two (b) Three (c) Four (d) Five

712. Which State in India has the largest area?
    (a) Madhya Pradesh (b) Uttar Pradesh (c) Maharashtra (d) Rajasthan

713. Which of the following States in India has the largest coastline?
    (a) Kerala (b) Orissa (c) Karnataka (d) Andhra Pradesh

714. How much of India's total land area is topographically usable?
    (a) 56% (b) 58% (c) 60% (d) 62%

715. What distance does India cover from north to south?
    (a) 2935 km (b) 3214 km (c) 3420 km (d) 3575 km

716. The length of India's coastline is:
    (a) 7517 km (b) 7625 km (c) 7715 km (d) 7847 km

717. How many islands are there in the Andaman and Nicobar group?
    (a) 182 (b) 223 (c) 238 (d) 246

718. Which Indian river is the longest?
    (a) Krishna (b) Ganga (c) Godavari (d) Narmada

719. Which place receives the highest rainfall in India?
    (a) Silchar (b) Sibsagar (c) Jorhat (d) Cherapunji

720. Into how many Indian States is the Thar Desert spread over?
    (a) One (b) Two (c) Three (d) Four

721. In the Himalayas, the highest peak within India is K2. Which is the second highest Indian peak?
(a) Nanda Devi (b) Nanga Parbat (c) Kamet (d) Kanchenjunga

722. On which river is Surat situated?
(a) Gomati (b) Godavari (c) Tapti (d) Betwa

723. What percentage of India's total land area is drained by the river Ganga?
(a) 15 (b) 20 (c) 25 (d) 30

724. Which is not a major *Kharif* crop in India?
(a) Rice (b) Wheat (c) Maize (d) Cotton

725. In which of the following States in India is the yield of forest wealth the highest per hectare?
(a) Madhya Pradesh (b) Uttar Pradesh (c) Kerala (d) Assam

726. How much of India's geographical area is subject to water and wind erosion?
(a) 135 million hectares (b) 145 million hectares (c) 165 million hectares (d) 182 million hectares

727. Which major soil group in India accounts for the largest geographical area?
(a) Red sandy soil (b) Medium black soil (c) Alluvial-recent soil (d) Red loamy soil

728. In which Indian State is soil erosion and land degradation the largest?
(a) Rajasthan (b) Andhra Pradesh (c) Madhya Pradesh (d) Gujarat

729. How much of India's total geographical area is forest land?
(a) 20% (b) 23% (c) 26% (d) 28%

730. In which State or Union Territory of India is the forest area highest as an percentage of total area?

(a) Arunachal Pradesh (b) Mizoram
(c) Andaman and Nicobar Islands (d) Tripura

731. In which year was Indian National Forest Policy formulated by the Government?
(a) 1948 (b) 1950 (c) 1952 (d) 1956

732. What is the percentage of the total land area in India which is to be brought under forests according to the National Forest Policy?
(a) 30 (b) 33 (c) 36 (d) 40

733. What is India's share in the total forest area of the world?
(a) 2% (b) 4% (c) 6% (d) 8%

734. Which of the following iron and steel plants in India are closer to coal fields than to iron ore deposits?
(a) Bhilai and Bokaro (b) Burnpur and Hirapur (c) Bhilai and Jamshedpur (d) Rourkela and Durgapur

735. By which river system in India is the Aravalli range bisected?
(a) Ghanga and Saraswati (b) Betwa and Sone
(c) Narmada and Manas (d) Tuni and Manas

736. At which of the following places are diamonds quarried in India?
(a) Panna (b) Kolar (c) Golconda
(d) Ankleshwar

737. How many principal hill ranges separate India from Burma?
(a) Two (b) Three (c) Four (d) Five

738. Which State in India has densely forested hills of strong sandstone, called the *Patkai Bum*?
(a) Tripura (b) Mizoram (c) Meghalaya
(d) Andhra Pradesh

739. In which state is Nalsarovar, a famous bird sanctuary of India, located?

(a) Gujarat (b) Rajasthan (c) Orissa
(d) Maharashtra

740. Identify the river on which the Hirakud Dam has been built:
(a) Godavari (b) Damodar (c) Sone
(d) Mahanadi

741. Which State in India has the largest coal reserves?
(a) Bihar (b) Orissa (c) Madhya Pradesh
(d) West Bengal

742. What is India's world rank in coal production?
(a) Seventh (b) Sixth (c) Fifth (d) Fourth

743. Which state has the largest resources of gypsum in India?
(a) Tamil Nadu (b) Rajasthan (c) Gujarat
(d) Andhra Pradesh

744. Approximately what percentage of petroleum consumption in India is supplied from domestic sources?
(a) 35 (b) 50 (c) 60 (d) 70

745. Although India imports a considerable quantity of oil, it has the distinction of having the second oldest oilfield in the world. Where is the oilfield located?
(a) Digboi (b) Duliajan (c) Nahorkatia
(d) Noonmati

746. Economic deposits of mica are found in three important belts in the country. Two of these are located in Andhra Pradesh and Bihar. Where is the third?
(a) Orissa (b) Rajasthan (c) Gujarat
(d) Madhya Pradesh

747. At present, how much of India's output of LPG comes from natural gas?
(a) 20% (b) 25% (c) 30% (d) 40%

748. Which State in India ranks at the bottom in rural electrification?
(a) Meghalaya (b) Arunachal Pradesh (c) Mizoram (d) Tripura

749. Coal mining in India was first started in 1774 at:
(a) Jharia (b) Singrauli (c) Ranigunj (d) Talcher

750. In which Indian State is lignite most abundantly found?
(a) Orissa (b) Karnataka (c) Tamil Nadu (d) Rajasthan

751. Which state in India produces the largest amount of mica?
(a) Bihar (b) Andhra Pradesh (c) Rajasthan (d) Orissa

752. Identify the chief industry located at Khetri:
(a) Newsprint (b) Copper (c) Aluminium (d) Zinc

753. Which of the following hydroelectric projects supplies electricity to the Rourkela Steel Plant?
(a) Damodar Valley Project (b) Nagarjuna Sagar Project (c) Hirakud Dam Project (d) Chambal Valley Project

754. Identify the State in India which depends primarily on thermal power:
West Bengal (b) Tamil Nadu (c) Maharashtra (d) Karnataka

755. Which of the following combinations is incorrect?
(a) Korba Thermal Power Station — Madhya Pradesh (b) Ramganga Project — Uttar Pradesh (c) Kosi Project — Bihar (d) Iddikki Project — Andhra Pradesh

X
INDIAN ECONOMY:
INSTITUTIONAL FRAMEWORK

756. When was the Minimum Wages Act enacted in the country?
(a) 1936 (b) 1948 (c) 1951 (d) 1956

757. When was the Indian Council of Agricultural Research established?
(a) 1947 (b) 1939 (c) 1935 (d) 1929

758. Where is the National Academy of Agricultural Research Management located?
(a) Dehra Dun (b) Hyderabad (c) New Delhi (d) Izatnagar

759. 'Operation Flood' is primarily concerned with:
(a) Flood Control (b) Dairy development
(c) Reclamation of marshy land (d) Development of fisheries

760. How many Finance Commissions have so far been set up in the country since the Constitution came into effect?
(a) Six (b) Seven (c) Eight (d) Eleven

761. Identify the State where *Panchayati Raj* was first introduced?
(a) Rajasthan (b) Maharashtra (c) Gujarat (d) Bihar

762. The National Institute of Port Management was set up in 1985. Where is it located?
(a) Calcutta (b) Madras (c) Bombay (d) Cochin

763. In which year was the Border Roads Development Board set up?
(a) 1956 (b) 1958 (c) 1960 (d) 1962

764. The Railway Staff College Conducts Courses in interdisciplinary subjects for offices. Where is it located?

(a) Pune (b) Vadodara (c) Jamalpur
(d) Secunderabad

765. The Integral Coach Factory is located at:
(a) Perambur (b) Varanasi (c) Calcutta
(d) Jabbalpur

766. The National Horticulture Board was set up
in 1984 to ensure the development of horticulture industry. Where are its headquarters?
(a) Shimla (b) Jammu (c) Gurgaon
(d) Tripura

767. Where is the Vaikunth Mehta National Institute of Co-operation Management located?
(a) Pune (b) Bombay (c) Nagpur
(d) Hyderabad

768. In which year was the integrated Rural
Development Programme initiated in the
country?
(a) 1977-78 (b) 1978-79 (c) 1979-80
(d) 1980-81

769. When was the All India Trade Union Congress
formed?
(a) 1919 (b) 1920 (c) 1921 (d) 1922

770. In which month of 1949 was the Reserve Bank
of India (RBI) nationalised?
(a) January (b) March (c) May (d) July

771. Where is the central office of the Life
Insurance Corporation of India (LIC) located?
(a) Delhi (b) Bombay (c) Calcutta (d) Madras

772. When was the Essential Commodities Act
enacted in the country?
(a) 1955 (b) 1956 (c) 1957 (d) 1958

773. Where is the Central Power Research Institute
located?
(a) Bangalore (b) Durgapur (c) New Delhi
(d) Nagpur

774. In which month of 1978 was the National Adult Education Programme launched in the country?
(a) January (b) April (c) August (d) October

775. How many vocational rehabilitation centres for the handicapped are functioning in the country?
(a) 17 (b) 19 (c) 21 (d) 23

776. Where is the Heavy Engineering Corporation Ltd located?
(a) Hyderabad (b) Ranchi (c) Bhopal (d) Bangalore

777. The Indian Petrochemical Corporation Ltd (IPCL) is located at:
(a) Baroda (b) Ahmedabad (c) Surat (d) Bhopal

778. Who was the Chairman of the National Income Committee set up in 1949?
(a) P.C. Mahalanobis (b) V.K.R.V. Rao (c) C.N. Vakil (d) K.N. Raj

779. The Community Development Programme ushered in an era of rural development with participation of the people. When was it launched?
(a) 1950 (b) 1952 (c) 1954 (d) 1956

780. Since when did the Save Grain Campaign become a regular scheme?
(a) 1965-66 (b) 1966-67 (c) 1967-68 (d) 1969-70

781. Where is the Central Agmark Laboratory located?
(a) Bombay (b) Calcutta (c) Madras (d) Nagpur

782. The Centrally sponsored District Industrial Centres (DICs) provide a focal point at the

district level for the promotion of small-scale and cottage industries. In which year was this programme launched?
(a) 1978 (b) 1980 (c) 1982 (d) 1984

783. In which year was the National Labour Institute set up by the Government?
(a) 1976 (b) 1972 (c) 1968 (d) 1964

784. How many Small Industries Service Institutes have been set up under the Small Industries Development Organisation (SIDO)?
(a) 21 (b) 23 (c) 25 (d) 27

785. When was the Lead Bank Scheme introduced in the country?
(a) 1971 (b) 1970 (c) 1969 (d) 1968

786. The principal objective of the State Trading Corporation (STC) is to diversify the country's foreign trade and to supplement efforts of private trade and industry in developing India's foreign trade. When was the STC set up?
(a) 1952 (b) 1956 (c) 1960 (d) 1966

787. Where is the Hindustan Teleprinters Ltd, a public sector undertaking engaged in the manufacture of telephones, ancillary equipment and electronic typewriters, located?
(a) Madras (b) Bangalore (c) Hyderabad (d) Dehra Dun

788. When was the National Co-operative Consumers' Federation set up to guide and promote the consumer co-operative movement in the country?
(a) 1961 (b) 1963 (c) 1965 (d) 1967

789. *Super Bazar*, the Co-operative Store Ltd, New Delhi, is one of the biggest co-operative institutions in the country. When was it established?

(a) 1964 (b) 1966 (c) 1968 (d) 1970

790. The Gas Authority of India Ltd, a wholly Government owned undertaking, was established in:
(a) 1984 (b) 1983 (c) 1982 (d) 1981

791. Oil exploration and production in India began in an extensive manner after the setting up of the Oil and Natural Gas Commission. When was this Commission set up?
(a) 1952 (b) 1954 (c) 1956 (d) 1958

792. The Centre for Agricultural Marketing is a pioneering national level organisation set up by the Union Government for offering specialised training, education and research activities in the field of agricultural marketing. Where is it located?
(a) Jaipur (b) New Delhi (c) Nagpur (d) Hyderabad

793. When did the Government acquire the shares of the Burma Oil Company?
(a) 1983 (b) 1982 (c) 1981 (d) 1980

794. When was the Central Consumer Protection Council constituted by the Union Government?
(a) 1987 (b) 1986 (c) 1985 (d) 1984

795. When was the National Thermal Power Corporation incorporated as a Public Sector Undertaking in India?
(a) 1977 (b) 1975 (c) 1973 (d) 1971

796. In which year was the Export Credit Guarantee Corporation of India set up?
(a) 1969 (b) 1971 (c) 1975

797. During 1989-90 two programmes were merged into one single rural employment

programme known as Jawahar Rozgar Yojna (JRY). RLEGP is one. Which is the other?
(a) IRDP (b) NREP (c) TRYSEM (d) DPAP

798. The Food Corporation of India (FCI) operates as the sole agency of the Central Government for procurement, import, distribution, storage, movement and sales of foodgrains. When was it set up?
(a) 1956 (b) 1960 (c) 1965 (d) 1970

799. Where is the National Fertiliser Ltd (NFL) located?
(a) Nangal (b) New Delhi (c) Philpur (d) Panipat

800. The Sponge Iron India Ltd (SIIL) is a joint undertaking of the Government of India and one State Government. Which one is it?
(a) Andhra Pradesh (b) Madhya Pradesh (c) Orissa (d) Goa

801. When was the Ministry of Programme Implementation, the management service arm of the Government of India, set up?
(a) 1985 (b) 1980 (c) 1974 (d) 1969

802. Where are the headquarters of the Trade Development Authority which was set up in July 1970?
(a) Chandigarh (b) Bombay (c) New Delhi (d) Ahmedabad

803. Where is the head office of the Forward Market Commission set up under the Forward Contracts (Regulation) Act of 1952?
(a) Bombay (b) New Delhi (c) Calcutta (d) Ahmedabad

804. Where is the National Handicrafts and Handlooms Museum located?

(a) Bangalore (b) Calcutta (c) Bombay
(d) New Delhi

805. How many industries have been included in Schedule 'A' of the Industrial Policy Resolution of 1956?
(a) 12 (b) 15 (c) 17 (d) 21

806. What name did Imperial Bank of India acquire after its nationalisation?
(a) Reserve Bank of India (b) State Bank of India (c) Central Bank of India (d) Bank of India

807. The national income estimates in the country are prepared by:
(a) National Income Committee (b) Planning Commission (c) Central Statistical Organisation (d) Reserve Bank of India

808. In which month does the Unit Trust of India (UTI) issue its units at concessional rates annually?
(a) January (b) March (c) July (d) October

809. Which of the following has the largest membership?
(a) Indian National Trade Union Congress (b) All India Trade Union Congress (c) Hind Mazdoor Sabha (d) United Trade Union Congress

810. The Employees State Insurance Act, 1948 marks the most important step in the provision of Social Security benefits in the country. It covers employees drawing monthly wages not exceeding:
(a) Rs 1200 (b) Rs 1400 (c) Rs 1600 (d) Rs 1800

811. The Equal Remuneration Act provides for payment of equal wages to men and women workers. When was it enacted?

(a) 1975 (b) 1976 (c) 1977 (d) 1978

812. The Rajghat Dam is an inter-state project between two States. One is Madhya Pradesh. Which is the other State?
(a) Rajasthan (b) Maharashtra (c) Gujarat (d) Uttar Pradesh

813. In which of the following sectors was the co-operative movement first initiated in the country?
(a) Agricultural credit (b) Agricultural marketing (c) Village and small-scale industries (d) Supply of agricultural inputs

814. The Central Water and Power Research Station is located at:
(a) Pune (b) New Delhi (c) Dehra Dun (d) Calcutta

815. The Department of Agricultural Research and Education is responsible for co-ordinating research and educational activities in the field of agriculture, animal husbandry and fisheries. When was it set up?
(a) 1973 (b) 1974 (c) 1975 (d) 1976

816. The Indian Airlines was established under the Air Corporation Act of 1953. Where are its headquarters?
(a) Bombay (b) Delhi (c) Calcutta (d) Madras

817. Which of the following was established first?
(a) Industrial Development Bank of India (b) Industrial Finance Corporation of India (c) Industrial Credit and Investment Corporation of India (d) Industrial Reconstruction Bank of India

818. When was the Companies Act enacted in the country?
(a) 1956 (b) 1958 (c) 1960 (d) 1962

819. Where are the headquarters of the Mineral Exploration Corporation Ltd. which was incorporated in 1972 to assess the mineral reserves of the country?
(a) Nagpur (b) Calcutta (c) Alwar (d) Hyderabad

820. Where are the headquarters of the Geological Survey of India?
(a) Nagpur (b) Dehra Dun (c) Calcutta (d) Bangalore

821. Where is the Indian Institute of Foreign Trade located?
(a) New Delhi (b) Hyderabad (c) Bombay (d) Ahmedabad

822. The Export Inspection Council is responsible for the enforcement of quality control and compulsory pre-shipment inspection of various exportable goods. Where is it located?
(a) Cochin (b) Calcutta (d) Madras (d) Bombay

823. The Export-Import Bank of India (Exim Bank) is the principal financial institution in the country for co-ordinating the working of institutions engaged in export financing and import trade. When was it established?
(a) 1976 (b) 1978 (c) 1980 (d) 1982

824. When was the first Agricultural Labour Enquiry conducted in the country?
(a) 1948-49 (b) 1949-50 (c) 1950-51 (d) 1951-52

825. The implementation of anti-poverty programmes in the country is closely monitored by the:
(a) Planning Commission (b) National Development Council (c) Ministry of Finance (d) Ministry of Programme Implementation

826. When was the Monopolies and Restrictive Trade Practices (MRTP) Act enacted?
(a) 1956 (b) 1961 (c) 1966 (d) 1969

827. In which year was the Industries Development and Regulation Act come into effect?
(a) 1956 (b) 1953 (c) 1951 (d) 1950

828. Which one of the following statements about the National Rural Employment Programme (NREP) is not correct?
(a) It was launched in October 1980 (b) It is a centrally sponsored schedule shared equally between Centre and States (c) It replaced the earlier 'food for work' programme (d) It provides for statutory guarantee of jobs

829. The Sarkaria Commission was appointed by the Central Government to review:
(a) Centre-State relations (b) Inter-State water disputes (c) Implementation of Punjab accord (d) Job reservation issues

830. Who was the Chairman of the Ninth Finance Commission?
(a) S.R. Sen (b) N.K.P. Salwe (c) L.K. Jha (d) Raja J. Chelliah

831. The Bharat Gold Mines Ltd (BGML) is the foremost producer of gold in the country. When was it incorporated?
(a) 1974 (b) 1972 (c) 1970 (d) 1968

832. The Cash Compensatory Scheme (CCS) is a scheme for:
(a) Export promotion (b) Industrial development (c) Encouraging workers to undertake risky jobs (d) Raising production

833. The Emigration Act regulates the emigration of citizens of India for employment in other countries. When was it enacted?

(a) 1980 (b) 1981 (c) 1982 (d) 1983

834. Central Cooperation Banks operate at the:
(a) National level (b) State level (c) District level (d) Village level

835. The apex bank for receiving agricultural credit is:
(a) NABARD (b) RBI (c) ARDC (d) SBI

836. The Exim Bank provides finance to:
(a) Large scale industries (b) Young entrepreneurs (c) Domestic commerce (d) Foreign trade

837. Which is the apex institution in the field of industrial finance in the country?
(a) IFC (b) IRBI (c) IDBI (d) ICICI

XI
INDIAN ECONOMIC ENVIRONMENT

838. The Indian economy can be most appropriately discribed as a:
(a) Capitalist economy (b) Socialist economy (c) Traditional economy (d) Mixed economy

839. What is India's world rank in population?
(a) First (b) Second (c) Third (d) Fourth

840. The annual addition to the country's population is almost equal to the total population of which of the following countries?
(a) Bangladesh (b) Australia (c) Bhutan (d) France

841. Which State in the country has the largest population?
(a) Uttar Pradesh (b) Maharashtra (c) Bihar (d) West Bengal

842. Which State in the country has the largest Scheduled Caste population?
(a) Uttar Pradesh (b) Bihar (c) West Bengal
(d) Tamil Nadu

843. In which State is the sex-ratio most favourable to females?
(a) Andhra Pradesh (b) Tamil Nadu (c) Kerala
(d) Karnataka

844. Which State in the country has the highest ratio of urban population?
(a) Maharashtra (b) Tamil Nadu (c) Gujarat
(d) Karnataka

845. Where is the work participation rate highest in the country?
(a) Arunachal Pradesh (b) Nagaland
(c) Andhra Pradesh (d) Sikkim

846. What is the percentage of working population in India, including both principal and marginal workers to the country's total population according to the 1981 census?
(a) 33.4 (b) 35.2 (c) 36.7 (d) 38.6

847. Which State shows the lowest infant mortality rate in the country?
(a) Punjab (b) Kerala (c) Andhra Pradesh
(d) Maharashtra

848. Which age-group in the country accounts for the highest percentage of total population?
(a) 0-9 years (b) 10-19 years (c) 20-29 years
(d) 30-39 years

849. Which State has the highest number of hospitals in the country?
(a) Kerala (b) Gujarat (c) Maharashtra
(d) Uttar Pradesh

850. In which State or Union Territory is the literacy rate highest in the country?

(a) Delhi (b) Chandigarh (c) Karnataka
(d) Kerala

851. Until which year was education the exclusive responsibility of States?
(a) 1960 (b) 1965 (c) 1970 (d) 1975

852. What is India's rank in the world of book publishing?
(a) Fourth (b) Fifth (c) Sixth (d) Seventh

853. When was the first agricultural census carried out in the country?
(a) 1960-61 (b) 1970-71 (c) 1975-76
(d) 1981-82

854. Approximately what percentage of the country's national income is derived from agriculture?
(a) 30 (b) 35 (c) 40 (d) 45

855. What percentage of the country's workforce is engaged in agriculture according to the 1981 census?
(a) 74.6 (b) 72.1 (c) 70.6 (d) 68.6

856. Small farmers in the country have been defined as those farmers having land holdings of:
(a) below 1 hectare (b) 1 to 2 hectare (c) 2 to 3 hectare (d) 3 to 4 hectare

857. Which of the following categories of agricultural holding account for the largest percentage of the total number of holdings in the country?
(a) Marginal holdings (b) Small holdings
(c) Medium holdings (d) Large holdings

858. Identify the State where fertiliser consumption per hectare of cropped area is the highest:
(a) Tamil Nadu (b) Andhra Pradesh
(c) Haryana (d) Punjab

859. Which of the following is the main source of irrigation in the country?
(a) Canals (b) Tanks (c) Wells (d) Rivers

860. Identify the State which has the largest share in the total production of groundnut in the country:
(a) Gujarat (b) Andhra Pradesh (c) Tamil Nadu (d) Karnataka

861. Which State has the largest net irrigated area as a percentage of net cropped area?
(a) Uttar Pradesh (b) Haryana (c) Tamil Nadu (d) Punjab

862. Which crop accounts for the largest area under cultivation in the country?
(a) Rice (b) Wheat (c) Pulses (c) Oilseeds

863. Which State is the largest producer of foodgrains in the country?
(a) Punjab (b) Uttar Pradesh (c) Madhya Pradesh (d) Andhra Pradesh

864. Which State has the largest share in the national production of rice?
(a) West Bengal (b) Bihar (c) Andhra Pradesh (d) Uttar Pradesh

865. Which State has the highest yield per hectare of wheat?
(a) Haryana (b) Punjab (c) Uttar Pradesh (d) Gujarat

866. What is India's rank in the world production of rice?
(a) First (b) Second (c) Third (c) Fourth

867. India ranks first in the world production of:
(a) Tea (b) Groundnut (b) Sugarcane (d) Cotton

868. India ranks third in the world in milk production. What is its rank in terms of per capita consumption of milk?
(a) 56th (b) 73rd (c) 84th (d) 93rd

869. Identify the first State in India to write off farmers' loans upto Rs 10,000 taken from public sector banks and regional rural banks:
(a) Goa (b) Haryana (c) Uttar Pradesh (d) Madhya Pradesh

870. In which year was the system of rationing introduced for the first time in the country?
(a) 1940-41 (b) 1943-44 (c) 1947-48 (d) 1949-50

871. What is India's ranking in the world in number of cattle?
(a) First (b) Second (c) Third (d) Fourth

872. When was the first Industrial Policy Statement made by the Government?
(a) 1947 (b) 1948 (c) 1949 (d) 1950

873. Where did the first State-owned fertiliser factory start production?
(a) Sindri (b) Nangal (c) Talcher (d) Gorakhpur

874. The first effort at large-scale production of iron and steel in the country got under way when Tata Iron and Steel Company was established in 1907. Where was it located?
(a) Jamshedpur (b) Kulti (c) Burnpur (d) Bhadravati

875. In which industry is the number of sick units the largest?
(a) Engineering (b) Textiles (c) Chemicals (d) Sugar

876. Which State has the distinction of having the largest number of registered small-scale industries?
(a) Tamil Nadu (b) West Bengal (c) Punjab (d) Maharastra

877. Which State has the largest number of factories?
(a) Tamil Nadu (b) Maharashtra (c) Gujarat (d) Andhra Pradesh

878. When did the *vanaspati* industry come into existence in the country?
(a) 1928 (b) 1930 (c) 1932 (d) 1934

879. Which of the following industries provides the largest number of employment in the country?
(a) Textile (b) Jute (c) Iron and steel (d) Sugar

880. What was the total number of running public enterprises of the Central Government at the commencement of the Seventh Plan in 1985-86?
(a) 202 (b) 207 (c) 211 (d) 214

881. The upper limit of investment in plant and machinery for small-scale industries has been fixed at:
(a) Rs 1 crore (b) Rs 50 lakh (c) Rs 45 lakh (d) Rs 35 lakh

882. What is India's world rank in the production of sugar?
(a) First (b) Second (c) Third (d) Fourth

883. When were the famous Kolar Gold Mines in the country nationalised?
(a) 1948 (b) 1956 (c) 1961 (d) 1965

884. In which State is the per capita domestic electricity consumption the lowest?
(a) Assam (b) Bihar (c) Rajasthan (d) Uttar Pradesh

885. As a railway system under single management, what rank does Indian Railways hold in the world?
(a) First (b) Second (c) Third (d) Fourth

886. What is approximately the total route kilometreage of the Indian Railways?
(a) 59,000 (b) 60,000 (c) 61,000 (d) 62,000

887. In which year did the first railway train steam off from Bombay to Thane, a stretch of 34 km?
(a) 1853 (b) 1855 (c) 1859 (d) 1861

888. Into how many zones are the Indian Railways divided?
(a) Ten (b) Nine (c) Eight (d) Seven

889. Since when were Railway finances separated from general finances?
(a) 1920-21 (b) 1924-25 (c) 1927-28 (d) 1934-35

890. Which is the fastest train in India?
(a) Frontier Mail (b) Rajdhani Express (c) Taj Express (d) Shatabdi Express

891. Railway locomotives in the country are built at two locations. One is Chittaranjan. Where is the other?
(a) Bangalore (b) Varanasi (c) Patiala (d) Perambur

892. Since when did State participation in road transport begin in the country?
(a) 1948 (b) 1950 (c) 1952 (d) 1954

893. Which State in the country has the greatest length of roads?
(a) Maharashtra (b) Tamil Nadu (c) Andhra Pradesh (d) Uttar Pradesh

894. What proportion of the total road length in the country is unsurfaced?
(a) 45% (b) 48% (c) 53% (d) 58%

895. Identify the State where cent per cent villages are connected with all-weather roads:

(a) Kerala (b) Punjab (c) Haryana (d) Gujarat

896. The Cochin Shipyard has been set up with the collaboration of a foreign country. Name the country:

(a) Japan (b) USA (c) USSR (d) West Germany

897. What is India's rank in the world in respect of shipping tonnage?

(a) Tenth (b) Twelfth (c) Fourteenth (d) Sixteenth

898. Which is India's biggest shipping line?

(a) Shipping Corporation of India Ltd. (b) Great Eastern Shipping Company Ltd. (c) India Steamship Company Ltd. (d) South India Shipping Corporation Ltd.

899. How many major ports are there in the country?

(a) eight (b) nine (c) ten (d) eleven

900. Which State leads in television coverage in terms of population?

(a) Punjab (b) West Bengal (c) Haryana (d) Tamil Nadu

901. Which State in the country has the lowest number of telephones per 1000 persons?

(a) Uttar Pradesh (b) Madhya Pradesh (c) Assam (d) Bihar

902. The International Subscriber Dialling (ISD) telephone service was first introduced from one Indian city to the UK. Which was that city?

(a) New Delhi (b) Bombay (c) Bangalore (d) Madras

903. When was the Postal Index Number (PIN), a numerical postal address code introduced in the country?
(a) 1970 (b) 1972 (c) 1974 (d) 1976

904. How many commercial banks were nationalished in India in 1980?
(a) Ten (b) Eight (c) Six (d) Four

905. Which State has the largest number of Regional Rural Banks?
(a) Uttar Pradesh (b) Andhra Pradesh (c) Maharashtra (d) Tamil Nadu

906. Identify the State or Union Territory where aggregate bank deposits are largest:
(a) West Bengal (b) Uttar Pradesh (c) Maharashtra (d) Delhi

907. The Tariff Aully for Major Ports started functioning from April
(a) 1994 (b) 1995 (c) 1996 (d) 1997

908. Where was a free trade zone created to promote the export of electronic goods from the country?
(a) Cochin (b) Haldia (c) Kandla (d) Marmugao

909. Which is India's most important export item at present?
(a) Tea (b) Engineering goods (c) Textiles (d) Handicrafts

910. On the import of which item do we spend the largest amount of foreign exchange?
(a) Petroleum oil and lubricants (b) Chemicals (c) Pearls, precious and semi-precious stones (d) Non-electrical machinery and appliances

911. Which country occupies the first place in India's foreign trade?
(a) USA (b) UK (c) Japan (d) Rusian Federation

912. As a member of the IMF, India pegged its currency initially with the pound sterling at a fixed parity rate. What was this rate?
(a) Re 1 = 1s (b) Re 1 = 1s 4d (c) Re 1 = 1s 6d (d) Re 1 = 1s 8d

913. The exchange value of the rupee is at present linked to:
(a) Gold only (b) US dollar (c) Yen (d) Multi-currency basket

914. When was decimal coinage introduced in India?
(a) 1955 (b) 1957 (d) 1959 (d) 1961

915. India has received the largest amount of foreign aid from:
(a) USA (b) IBRD (c) IBA (d) USSR

916. How much of the country's total tax revenue is raised through indirect taxes?
(a) 86% (b) 82% (c) 75% (d) 70%

917. On which of the following items does the Central Government incur the laigest amount of non-development expenditure?
(a) Defence (b) Interest payments (c) Subsidies (d) General services

918. Which of the following categories brings the maximum amount of revenue receipts to the Government in India?
(a) Indirect taxes (b) Direct taxes (c) Net contribution by public undertakings (d) Non-tax revenues

919. Which of the following is not a source of revenue to the Union Government?
(a) Customs (b) Agricultural income tax (c) Wealth tax (d) Corporation tax

920. As a percentage of gross domestic product, the total tax revenue in the country is:

(a) 14 (b) 15 (c) 16 (d) 17

921. The Government has accumulated huge stocks of smuggled gold seized by enforcement agencies in the country. The value of this gold is estimated to be:
(a) Rs 7,500 crore (b) Rs 10,000 crore (c) Rs 12,500 crore (d) Rs 15,000 crore

922. Which of the following is the most important source of revenue of the State Governments in India?
(a) Sales tax (b) Share of union excise duty (c) Land revenue (d) Entertainment tax

XII

PLANNING AND DEVELOPMENT IN INDIA

923. *Planned Economy for India*, published in 1934, is said to have initiated discussion on the need for planning in the country. Identify the author of this work:
(a) V.K.R.V. Rao (b) C.N. Vakil (c) M. Visveswariah (d) M.N. Roy

924. Who was the Chairman of the National Planning Committee set up in 1938 by the Indian National Congress?
(a) Jawaharlal Nehru (b) Subhas Chandra Bose (c) Asaf Ali (d) J.B. Kripalani

925. How many leading industrialists joined together to formulate a fifteen year plan for India's economic development which came to be known as the Bombay Plan?
(a) Five (b) Six (c) Seven (d) Eight

926. Who formulated the People's Plan for India in 1944?

(a) Jawaharlal Nehru (b) M.N. Roy (c) Subhas Chandra Bose (d) Mahatma Gandhi

927. When was the Planning Commission set up to prepare the blueprint for development taking an overall view of the needs and resources of the country?
(a) 1948 (b) 1949 (c) 1950 (d) 1951

928. Who is the ex-officio Chairman of the Planning Commission?
(a) Finance Minister (b) Prime Minister (c) Deputy Prime Minister (d) Minister for Planning

929. The First Five Year Plan was launched on:
(a) 26 January 1950 (b) 1 April 1950 (c) 1 January 1951 (d) 1 April 1951

930. In which Plan was self-reliance first emphasised?
(a) Second Plan (b) Third Plan (c) Fourth Plan (d) Fifth Plan

931. Which Five Year Plan was terminated one year earlier than its scheduled end?
(a) Third Plan (b) Fourth Plan (c) Fifth Plan (d) Sixth Plan

932. As a percentage of the total plan outlay, in which Five-Year Plan has investment in health been highest?
(a) First Plan (b) Third Plan (c) Fifth Plan (d) Seventh Plan

933. The realised annual growth rate during the First Plan was 3.6% (at 1980-81 prices) as against the target of:
(a) 2.1% (b) 2.5% (c) 3.2% (d) 4.0%

934. What was the duration of the Sixth Five Year Plan?

(a)   1978-83   (b)   1979-84   (c)   1980-85
(d) 1981-86

935. Under which Five Year Plan was the envisaged dependence on deficit financing for mobilising plan resources the largest?
(a) Second Plan (b) Third Plan (c) Fourth Plan (d) Sixth Plan

936. In which Plan did external assistance rank topmost as a source of financing?
(a) Second Plan (b) Third Plan (c) Annual Plans (d) Fifth Plan

937. In which Five Year Plan was transport and communication accorded the highest priority in terms of the percentage allocation of the plan-outlay?
(a) First Plan (b) Second Plan (c) Third Plan (d) Fourth Plan

938. In which Five Year Plan was percentage share of plan-outlay on power the highest?
(a) Third Plan (b) Fourth Plan (c) Fifth Plan (d) Sixth Plan

939. Identify the year during which the net national product increased by about 11% at 1980-81 prices:
(a)   1988-89   (b)   1983-84   (c)   1980-81
(d) 1967-68

940. By which year is the goal 'Health for All' to be achieved in the country?
(a) 1996 (b) 2000 (c) 2005 (d) 2010

941. The expectation of life at birth in the country shows considerable improvement since Independence. It was around 32 years during 1941-50. What was the expectation of life at birth during 1981-86?

129

(a) 48 years (b) 52 years (c) 54 years
(d) 56 years

942. The number of hospitals and dispensaries in the country have been steadily rising. From nearly 9,600 in 1950, it increased to 13,900 in 1960. What was their number in 1988?

(a) 39,000 (b) 35,600 (c) 30,500 (d) 27,800

943. In which Five Year Plan was the clinical approach to family planning supplemented by the extension approach?

(a) Second Plan (b) Third Plan (c) Fourth Plan
(d) Fifth Plan

944. The hospital bed to population ratio was 0.24 per thousand at the time of the commencement of the First Plan. What is approximately the ratio now?

(A) 1.42 (b) 1.12 (c) 0.72 (d) 0.54

945. The death rate in India has fallen fairly rapidly since Independence. From 27.4 per thousand in 1971. What was the estimated death rate in 1987-88?

(a) 13.2 (b) 12.4 (c) 11.6 (d) 10.8

946. The literacy rate in the country, though low, has been steadily rising. From 16.7% in 1951, it rose to 29.5% in 1971. What was the literacy rate in 1981?

(a) 34.4% (b) 36.2% (c) 37.6% (d) 39.4%

947. The Resolution on National Policy of Education was adopted in

(a) 1966 (b) 1968 (c) 1970 (d) 1972

948. Which decade of Indian planning has been the best for agricultural growth?

(a) Fifties (b) Sixties (c) Seventies (d) Eighties

949. The Green Revolution refers to the dramatic increase in agricultural production in a short period of time around the mid-sixties. With which crop has it been mainly associated?

(a) Wheat (b) Rice (c) Cotton (d) Sugarcane

950. Under British rule, India's agriculture remained largely in a state of stagnation. What was the estimated annual growth rate in agricultural production during the first half of the twentieth century?

(a) 1.25% (b) 0.75% (C) 0.50% (d) 0.25%

951. Though subject to large periodic fluctuations, agricultural production in the country exhibits a definite upward trend since the commencement of planning. What is the average growth rate per annum?

(a) 3.5% (b) 2.7% (c) 2.2% (d) 1.8%

952. In which year since 1951 has the per capita net availability of cereals been the highest in the country?

(a) 1965 (b) 1972 (c) 1984 (d) 1989

953. The long-term trend in respect of per capita net availability of pulses in the country has been:

(a) Increasing (b) Decreasing (c) Widely fluctuating (d) Almost constant

954. Agricultural production recorded the highest increase in the Sixth Plan. What was the annual rate of growth?

(a) 4% (b) 5% (c) 6% (d) 7%

955. In which year of the eighties did the production of food grains establish a new record of 170.3 million tonnes?

(a) 1988-89 (b) 1985-86 (c) 1984-85
(d) 1983-84

956. Under which Five Year Plan did agricultural production record a negative growth?
(a) Second Plan (b) Third Plan (c) Fourth Plan
(d) Fifth Plan

957. In one particular year during 1978-79 to 1988-89 India's imports recorded a rise of as much as 37,3%. Which year was it?
(a) 1979-80 (b) 1980-81 (c) 1985-86
(d) 1988-89

958. The average size of agricultural holdings has been steadily decreasing over time. It stood at 3.1 hectare in 1953-54 and 2.3 hectare in 1970-71. What is the estimate of the average size relating to the year 1985-86?
(a) 2 hectare (b) 1.8 hectare (c) 1.6 hectare
(d) 1.4 hectare

959. Under which Five Year Plan was the annual growth rate of exports the highest?
(a) Seventh Plan (b) Sixth Plan (c) Fifth Plan
(d) Fourth Plan

960. The annual growth rate of imports during the Fifth Plan was highest at:
(a) 16.5% (b) 20.5% (c) 18.5% (d) 19.5%

961. Under which Five Year Plan was the annual growth rate of bank deposits the highest?
(a) Third Plan (b) Fourth Plan (c) Fifth Plan
(d) Sixth Plan

962. The annual growth rate in industrial production was highest under the:
(a) Second Plan (b) Third Plan (c) Fifth Plan
(d) Sixth Plan

963. Identify the Five Year Plan during which the growth rate in industrial production happened to be the lowest:
(a) First Plan (b) Second Plan (c) Fourth Plan (d) Fifth Plan

964. During the Seventh Plan period industry grew at an annual compound rate of:
(a) 7.8% (b) 9% (c) 10.2% (d) 8.4%

965. Identify the year during which wholesale prices in the country registered a record rise of over 25%:
(a) 1973-74 (b) 1974-75 (c) 1979-80 (d) 1980-81

966. During the period of the First Plan prices showed a declining trend. What was the annual rate of decline in prices over this period?
(a) 1.5% (b) 2.2% (c) 2.7% (d) 3.1%

967. Which of the following commodities has shown the fastest rise in prices since the seventies?
(a) Cement (b) Coal (c) Iron and steel (d) Pulses

968. The purchasing power of the Rupee has been falling quite rapidly. At 1960-61 prices, it stood at 60 paisa in 1968-69 and at 30 paisa in 1978-79. What was its purchasing power in paisa ten years later in 1988-89?
(a) 16 (b) 15 (c) 14 (d) 13

969. Under which Plan did wholesale prices record the largest increase?
(a) Seventh Plan (b) Sixth Plan (c) Fifth Plan (d) Fourth Plan

970. India's adverse balance of trade has been increasing rapidly since 1979-80. In which of the following years was the adverse trade balance highest?

(a) 1983-84 (b) 1985-86 (c) 1986-87
(d) 1988-89

971. In only two years since 1949-50 India has had a favourable trade balance. 1972-73 was one such year. The other year was:
(a) 1955-56 (b) 1968-69 (d) 1976-77
(d) 1978-79

972. Since 1960-61 India's exports decreased in two particular years. 1965-66 was one such year. The other year was:
(a) 1975-76 (b) 1980-81 (c) 1985-86
(d) 1987-88

973. In which State or Union Territory is the share of priority sectors in total bank credit the largest?
(a) Haryana (b) Tripura (c) Punjab
(d) Manipur

974. The length of surfaced roads in the country has increased from 1.6 lakh km in 1950-51 to 8.3 lakh km in 1988-89. What is approximately the percentage of villages connected with all-weather roads?
(a) 28 (b) 31 (c) 33 (d) 36

975. Which of the following statistics in the transport sector shows the highest annual growth rate during the period of planning?
(a) International air passenger traffic (b) Domestic air passenger traffic (c) Overseas shipping tonnage (d) Railways' electrified route length

976. In which year did Parliament declare that the broad objective of economic policy should be to achieve a socialistic pattern in society?
(a) 1950 (b) 1952 (c) 1954 (d) 1956

977. In which Five-Year Plan was rapid industrialisation, with particular emphasis on the development of basic and heavy industries, laid down as one of the principal objectives?
(a) First Plan (b) Second Plan (c) Third Plan (d) Fourth Plan

978. The First Five Year Plan completed its period in 1956. When did the Fourth Five Year Plan begin?
(a) 1966 (b) 1967 (c) 1968 (d) 1969

979. In which State was the per capita plan outlay lowest under the Sixth Plan?
(a) Assam (b) Bihar (c) Orissa (d) Rajasthan

980. Which is the highest body that approves Five-Year Plans in the country?
(a) Planning Commission (b) Union Cabinet (c) National Development Council (d) Parliament

981. Which of the following received the highest allocation of resources in the Seventh Plan?
(a) Agriculture and irrigation (b) Energy and power (b) Social services (d) Industry and minerals

982. During which Five Year Plan did the per capita income register the largest increase on an annual basis?
(a) Seventh Plan (b) Sixth Plan (c) Fifth Plan (d) Fourth Plan

983. Though marked by frequent ups and downs, per capita income in the country shows a rising trend. What was the average annual growth rate during 1951-86?
(a) 0.9% (b) 1.3% (c) 1.5% (d) 2.1%

984. What was the average annual growth rate in national income during the period 1951-86?

135

(a) 2.6% (b) 3.0% (c) 3.5% (d) 4%

985. Since the commencement of planning, gross domestic savings as per cent of gross domestic product, reached its highest level in 1978-79 at:

(a) 21.2% (b) 21.8% (c) 22.6% (d) 23.2%

986. In which year since 1950-51 did gross domestic capital formation, as per cent of gross domestic product at current prices, reach its highest level of 23.9%?

(a) 1988-89 (b) 1985-86 (c) 1980-81 (d) 1978-79

987. During which Five Year Plan was the overall incremental capital-output ratio found to be the lowest?

(a) First Plan (b) Second Plan (c) Third Plan (d) Fifth Plan

988. In which plan did the overall incremental capital-output ratio turn out to be the highest?

(a) Seventh Plan (b) Sixth Plan (c) Fourth Plan (d) Third Plan

989. Under which Five Year Plan was the annual growth rate in national income, at 1980-81 prices, the lowest?

(a) Fourth Plan (b) Third Plan (c) Second Plan (d) First Plan

990. The actual growth rate at 1980-81 prices during the Fifth Plan period was 4.9% per annum. Identify the target laid down in the plan:

(a) 4% (b) 4.4% (c) 5% (d) 5.2%

991. Which three-year period was observed as a plan holiday in the country?

(a) 1965-68 (b) 1966-69 (c) 1968-71 (d) 1969-72

992. What annual growth rate target in respect of national income was laid down in the Third Plan?
(a) 4.2% (b) 4.8% (c) 5.2% (d) 5.6%

993. What is the target for the reduction of poverty in the country by AD 2000?
(a) 15% (b) 10% (c) 7% (d) 5%

994. Which State had the lowest proportion of population below the poverty line in 1983-84?
(a) Punjab (b) Manipur (c) Kerala (d) Himachal Pradesh

995. In which State was the proportion of population below the poverty line highest in 1983-84?
(a) Bihar (b) Madhya Pradesh (c) Orissa (d) Uttar Pradesh

996. The population below poverty line in the country in 1983-84 stood at 37.4%. What was this percentage in respect of Scheduled Tribes in that year?
(a) 57.1 (b) 55.4 (c) 50.9 (d) 48.2

997. The poverty rate in urban areas in 1984-85 was estimated at about 28%. What was the estimated rate for rural areas in that year?
(a) 50% (b) 45% (c) 40% (d) 35%

998. During which Five Year Plan was the Minimum Needs Programme launched in the country?
(a) Second Plan (b) Fourth Plan (c) Fifth Plan (d) Sixth Plan

999. Since the commencement of planning in 1951-52, the per capita income at 1980-81 prices recorded a decrease of over 6% in two particular years. 1965-66 was one such year. The other year was:

(a)   1957-58   (b)   1972-73   (c)   1979-80
(d) 1982-83

1000. The per capita daily income in the country at 1980-81 prices was Rs 3 at the beginning of the First Plan in 1950-51. Identify this amount at the commencement of the Seventh Plan in 1985-86:

(a) Rs 4.6 (b) Rs 4.8 (c) Rs 5 (d) Rs 5.4

ANSWERS

1. d	2. c	3. b	4. a	5. c
6. b	7. c	8. b	9. b	10. c
11. a	12. b	13. a	14. b	15. a
16. a	17. b	18. c	19. a	20. a
21. b	22. d	23. b	24. d	25. a
26. c	27. c	28. b	29. b	30. d
31. b	32. c	33. b	34. b	35. a
36. c	37. a	38. b	39. b	40. b
41. c	42. a	43. b	44. a	45. a
46. d	47. a	48. b	49. a	50. b
51. c	52. b	53. a	54. b	55. b
56. a	57. a	58. d	59. a	60. d
61. b	62. c	63. a	64. a	65. a
66. a	67. c	68. a	69. a	70. a
71. b	72. c	73. a	74. d	75. a
76. b	77. d	78. c	79. d	80. d
81. d	82. b	83. a	84. b	85. c
86. d	87. a	88. b	89. a	90. b
91. b	92. b	93. c	94. c	95. d
96. b	97. b	98. d	99. c	100. d
101. a	102. b	103. d	104. c	105. a
106. a	107. b	108. a	109. a	110. b
111. c	112. d	113. b	114. d	115. d
116. d	117. d	118. b	119. d	120. c
121. b	122. a	123. d	124. a	125. a
126. c	127. d	128. d	129. b	130. a
131. c	132. d	133. b	134. b	135. a
136. c	137. d	138. d	139. d	140. d

141. a	142. a	143. c	144. a	145. b
146. d	147. b	148. d	149. a	150. b
151. d	152. a	153. c	154. b	155. b
156. b	157. d	158. a	159. d	160. c
161. b	162. c	163. a	164. d	165. b
166. a	167. d	168. d	169. c	170. d
171. d	172. d	173. a	174. d	175. b
176. c	177. d	178. a	179. b	180. b
181. b	182. a	183. d	184. d	185. c
186. a	187. c	188. a	189. c	190. a
191. c	192. c	193. d	194. d	195. c
196. c	197. a	198. b	199. b	200. d
201. b	202. c	203. b	204. c	205. a
206. d	207. c	208. b	209. c	210. d
211. b	212. a	213. a	214. c	215. b
216. c	217. a	218. b	219. b	220. b
221. c	222. a	223. d	224. a	225. b
226. a	227. a	228. b	229. b	230. a
231. b	232. b	233. c	234. b	235. b
236. c	237. b	238. b	239. a	240. a
241. c	242. a	243. a	244. b	245. c
246. c	247. d	248. c	249. b	250. a
251. d	252. b	253. c	254. a	255. b
256. b	257. c	258. d	259. d	260. d
261. d	262. c	263. d	264. b	265. c
266. b	267. b	268. b	269. b	270. c
271. c	272. b	273. a	274. b	275. b
276. c	277. d	278. c	279. d	280. c
281. a	282. c	283. c	284. a	285. b
286. a	287. d	288. d	289. d	290. a

291. b	292. a	293. c	294. c	295. b
296. b	297. d	298. d	299. b	300. d
301. a	302. a	303. a	304. a	305. d
306. d	307. a	308. b	309. a	310. b
311. d	312. a	313. d	314. d	315. b
316. c	317. b	318. a	319. c	320. b
321. a	322. d	323. c	324. d	325. b
326. d	327. b	328. c	329. d	330. d
331. c	332. a	333. a	334. b	335. a
336. d	337. d	338. c	339. b	340. a
341. b	342. b	343. d	344. b	345. a
346. c	347. c	348. b	349. c	350. c
351. b	352. d	353. a	354. b	355. b
356. a	357. d	358. a	359. a	360. d
361. b	362. a	363. b	364. d	365. b
366. c	367. a	368. a	369. d	370. d
371. d	372. a	373. b	374. a	375. a
376. b	377. a	378. b	379. d	380. b
381. b	382. c	383. d	384. a	385. c
386. b	387. c	388. c	389. b	390. c
391. b	392. d	393. b	394. b	395. a
396. b	397. b	398. d	399. d	400. c
401. c	402. b	403. d	404. d	405. b
406. c	407. c	408. b	409. a	410. d
411. b	412. a	413. b	414. d	415. a
416. b	417. d	418. c	419. d	420. b
421. c	422. d	423. a	424. b	425. b
426. d	427. d	428. c	429. b	430. a
431. a	432. b	433. b	434. c	435. c
436. d	437. c	438. a	439. b	440. c

441. b	442. b	443. c	444. c	445. b
446. c	447. a	448. a	449. b	450. a
451. b	452. c	453. b	454. b	455. c
456. d	457. d	458. a	459. b	460. b
461. a	462. c	463. b	464. b	465. b
466. a	467. c	468. a	469. a	470. c
471. b	472. a	473. d	474. b	475. b
476. c	477. a	478. b	479. b	480. b
481. a	482. b	483. a	484. c	485. b
486. b	487. a	488. b	489. a	490. a
491. c	492. d	493. a	494. b	495. a
496. b	497. c	498. c	499. c	500. a
501. c	502. c	503. d	504. b	505. a
506. b	507. a	508. c	509. d	510. b
511. a	512. c	513. d	514. a	515. d
516. b	517. d	518. c	519. a	520. c
521. c	522. c	523. a	524. b	525. d
526. a	527. a	528. d	529. a	530. c
531. c	532. a	533. c	534. a	535. c
536. c	537. b	538. d	539. a	540. c
541. d	542. d	543. a	544. c	545. d
546. c	547. b	548. d	549. b	550. d
551. b	552. c	553. d	554. d	555. b
556. a	557. d	558. b	559. c	560. d
561. d	562. d	563. d	564. c	565. a
566. c	567. c	568. b	569. a	570. c
571. b	572. a	573. b	574. b	575. c
576. a	577. b	578. d	579. b	580. a
581. b	582. c	583. b	584. b	585. c
586. d	587. c	588. d	589. d	590. b

591. c	592. a	593. c	594. b	595. a
596. b	597. a	598. d	599. c	600. a
601. c	602. b	603. a	604. d	605. a
606. b	607. c	608. d	609. c	610. b
611. d	612. d	613. c	614. a	615. b
616. d	617. b	618. d	619. b	620. b
621. c	622. a	623. d	624. b	625. a
626. d	627. a	628. c	629. b	630. a
631. b	632. a	633. b	634. c	635. a
636. b	637. b	638. a	639. c	640. a
641. c	642. d	643. c	644. b	645. b
646. d	647. a	648. b	649. d	650. c
651. b	652. d	653. c	654. b	655. c
656. a	657. a	658. c	659. c	660. b
661. b	662. b	663. b	664. b	665. d
666. b	667. b	668. a	669. c	670. a
671. c	672. a	673. d	674. b	675. c
676. a	677. d	678. a	679. b	680. a
681. d	682. c	683. d	684. d	685. b
686. b	687. d	688. b	689. a	690. a
691. d	692. a	693. b	694. a	695. c
696. b	697. d	698. a	699. c	700. b
701. c	702. b	703. b	704. b	705. a
706. b	707. b	708. a	709. c	710. c
711. b	712. a	713. d	714. d	715. b
716. a	717. b	718. b	719. d	720. d
721. d	722. c	723. c	724. b	725. d
726. b	727. a	728. a	729. b	730. a
731. c	732. b	733. a	734. b	735. d
736. a	737. b	738. d	739. a	740. d

741. a	742. d	743. b	744. d	745. a
746. b	747. c	748. b	749. c	750. c
751. a	752. b	753. c	754. a	755. d
756. b	757. d	758. b	759. b	760. d
761. a	762. b	763. c	764. b	765. a
766. c	767. a	768. b	769. b	770. a
771. b	772. a	773. a	774. d	775. a
776. b	777. a	778. a	779. b	780. d
781. d	782. a	783. b	784. d	785. c
786. b	787. a	788. c	789. b	790. a
791. c	792. a	793. c	794. a	795. b
796. b	797. b	798. c	799. b	800. a
801. a	802. c	803. c	804. d	805. c
806. b	807. c	808. c	809. a	810. c
811. c	812. d	813. a	814. a	815. a
816. b	817. b	818. a	819. a	820. c
821. a	822. b	823. d	824. c	825. d
826. d	827. c	828. d	829. a	830. b
831. c	832. a	833. d	834. c	835. a
836. d	837. c	838. d	839. b	840. b
841. a	842. a	843. c	844. a	845. a
846. c	847. b	848. a	849. a	850. d
851. d	852. d	853. b	854. b	855. c
856. b	857. b	858. d	859. c	860. b
861. d	862. a	863. b	864. a	865. b
866. b	867. a	868. d	869. a	870. b
871. a	872. b	873. a	874. a	875. a
876. b	877. b	878. b	879. a	880. c
881. a	882. b	883. b	884. b	885. b
886. d	887. a	888. b	889. b	890. d

891. b	892. b	893. a	894. c	895. a
896. a	897. d	898. a	899. d	900. a
901. d	902. b	903. b	904. c	905. a
906. c	907. d	908. c	909. d	910. a
911. a	912. c	913. d	914. b	915. b
916. a	917. b	918. a	919. b	920. d
921. b	922. a	923. c	924. a	925. d
926. b	927. c	928. b	929. d	930. c
931. c	932. a	933. a	934. c	935. a
936. c	937. b	938. c	939. a	940. b
941. d	942. a	943. b	944. c	945. d
946. b	947. b	948. d	949. a	950. d
951. b	952. d	953. b	954. c	955. a
956. b	957. b	958. c	959. a	960. d
961. c	962. b	963. c	964. d	965. b
966. c	967. b	968. d	969. b	970. b
971. c	972. c	973. d	974. d	975. a
976. c	977. b	978. d	979. b	980. c
981. b	982. a	983. c	984. c	985. d
986. a	987. a	988. a	989. b	990. b
991. b	992. d	993. d	994. b	995. a
996. a	997. c	998. c	999. c	1000. c